A Third Cell
in America

A Third Cell in America

A Novel

Richard D. Ondo,
author of *Terror by Invasion*

iUniverse, Inc.
New York Lincoln Shanghai

A Third Cell in America

iUniverse books may be ordered through booksellers or by contacting:

iUniverse
2021 Pine Lake Road, Suite 100
Lincoln, NE 68512
www.iuniverse.com
1-800-Authors (1-800-288-4677)

Because of the dynamic nature of the Internet, any Web addresses or links contained in this book may have changed since publication and may no longer be valid.

This is a work of fiction. All of the characters, names, incidents, organizations, and dialogue in this novel are either the products of the author's imagination or are used fictitiously.

ISBN: 978-0-595-44434-2 (pbk)
ISBN: 978-0-595-88761-3 (ebk)

Printed in the United States of America

Prologue

The mysticism of Richard Stern's dreams is of great importance to the FBI. His brush with real FBI agents stimulates an idea. Stern, a risk taker, seeks a means to improve his bottom line. His new profession, he claims to be a bounty hunter. He purchases a small caliber pistol as an equalizer hoping to improve his safety.

His personal habit, alcohol, is an unlikely servant, serving up visions, dreams, and hallucinations that signal terrorist plans. He uses booze, as it is a key to unlock the secrets of the enemy. The spirits are a shallow friend and his ticket to trouble. Richard Stern's dreams turn out to be a living nightmare.

Rehabilitation at a local hospital was not enough to keep him from the bottle. Stern sets out to identify terrorist cells on his own. Alcohol emboldens him to move very close to the enemy.

Stern's habitual weakness and bumbling is a testament to his foolish attempt at bounty hunting terrorists. He is fortunate FBI agents are nearby.

A criminal act occurs at a rural farming village near Lake Erie. North Perry, home to a nuclear power plant in Middle America, is rocked by an explosion. Deputy Sheriffs realize the terrorists never abandoned the plot to assault the Perry Nuclear Power Plant. The first failed attempt six months prior ended up with many arrests. The ringleader, Mr. Big, escaped. He has not given up on causing terror. His patience and determination is tested after a car bomb explodes killing three female terrorists. With the elimination of the second cell another target of national interest is chosen.

Other hidden terrorist cells have been lying dormant. The Third Cell would be called into action by the ringleader. A THIRD CELL IN AMERICA takes roots.

The diabolical schemers are piercing North America. The fight by seasoned crime fighters is joined by an unlikely vigilante. His novice approach at espionage provides a glimmer of hope about terrorist activities. Terrorists are along the shores of Lake Erie. The third cell leader is on the threshold of building a new delivery system. Working at a feverish pace, the terrorists must overcome the probing and constant gains made by Homeland Security.

A trio of terrorist masterminds begins work on a more sinister operation. Extensive preparations are planned by Mr. Big, the chief terrorist in North America. His operations lieutenant, Captain Awad and third cell leader, Klalil Mahdi, grow more dangerous each day. Klalil Mahdi disposes of his first laboratory and opens a larger pilot operation. The plan is to expand the cells in Middle America. A terrorist future plan is slightly illuminated in Buffalo, New York as a terrorist laboratory is discovered. Stumbling on the evidence is Richard Stern.

1

The Second Coming

With our nation at war in Iraq, the attempted sneak attack from our northern border adds tension to an already nervous America. Our homeland defense is heightened by the sheer boldness of the failed American attack last July. Search parties of home grown mercenaries and bounty hunters have joined in the hunt for the terrorists who slipped through the police dragnet. The FBI and local sheriffs have put up posters of the wanted terrorist. No longer is America that concerned about court justice. Street justice for a terrorist has become the rule. A form of wild-west fever, dead or alive bravado, is gripping the nation.

Americans are rolling up their sleeves gearing up for a homeland defense. Instructions and training are administered by newly formed civil defense teams. Precautionary instructions are taught to guard against biological warfare. A real war footing has taken hold. Towns across America find comfort in local associations such as the VFW, the American Legion and local church groups.

Americans decide homeland terrorism is a real war and has real consequences. A traitor will be executed. Anyone even considering joining an anti-American cause will be added to the deport list. American judges are handing out stern messages by sentencing hard criminals to maximum incarceration. Even the Liberal Party has stopped crying about secret CIA prisons. Civil liberty organizations are told to dummy up already. Buy American is the news. Americans demand American oil be used and the hell with the Middle Eastern crude. American oil companies ramp up exploration in American territories.

Richard Stern is engaged in a conversation with two girls. He is shy and uses the alcohol to overcome that weakness. Their ample curves, makes him wish he was young again. This is a perfect opportunity. He will instruct them in the dangers of alcohol abuse. This fact has been a weakness and sickness Richard has fought all his life. His conversation turns to his own alcoholism.

"Girls, I lack the willpower to surrender my alcoholic ways," he concedes.

"You may not have the same genes in your bodies as I do," he laments.

"Yes we do Richard, see." The pretty girl hops off the bar stool and bends over revealing a tight pair of jeans on a well formed bottom. Her hands rub the blue cotton denim that is straining to contain a seductive set of buns.

"You girls don't care. You just turned twenty-one. It is your turn to learn the ropes," Richard calmly speaks. He lives the alcoholic life style. He has seen the long term effects of alcohol abuse. He refuses to tackle his own problem.

He downs another drink wishing it would be his last. He's drenched in guilt about his failure to warn the public about his suspicion and visions of terrorists. Indeed, his drinking problem has gripped him emotionally. He continues to cross examine himself. He finally settles his anguish by rationalizing that his visions come from the booze. He downs another beer and becomes more intoxicated.

Stern did help save the day. He worked up the whiskey courage to visit the Cleveland FBI and inform Agent Ron Roman of his mysterious dreams. That was months ago. The timing of that visit coincided with another warning from a citizen. Agent Roman didn't ignore the implications. Later, Agent Roman and Agent Bill Wright visited Stern in the hospital. Stern's alcoholism ended up aiding the FBI. The terrorist plan unraveled for the FBI to see. The booze played a role in the outcome. It also kept Stern from enjoying the huge terrorist bust. Stern's stay in the hospital and brief recovery was not enough to keep him from the bars.

"I tipped them off so they were able to pick apart these diabolical schemers. I can drink again because I'll see the future, but this time, I'll get the word out early to save our nation from the next attack," he mumbles.

"That's it, I've had enough,"

"I didn't drive the van tonight. I got the message about drinking and driving."

Richard walks slowly out of the bar, somewhat stiff legged. As he crosses the threshold, he stumbles but maintains his balance. Richard hears a whisper from St. Jude,

"*Richard, you are at the mercy of alcohol.*"

"Somehow, I need to get back into AA," Richard confesses.

"If only I wouldn't take that first drink."

Richard walks a few blocks towards Lake Erie. The lake is about a half mile away. He has good reason to go this way. He can stop at a couple more bars along the way. In his drunken state, it's the natural thing to do. He slows down and looks into the window of a tavern.

"Yep, there's Mel, Andy, and Bob," he says.

Richard sees the same drunks in the smoke filled bar. He enters the rundown bar and finds a bar stool between several regulars.

"No one wanted that stool because it's off balance and rocks around," says Mel.

"The stool is like me, Mel. People avoid me. They call me a drunk. I'll prove them wrong this time," Richard explains.

"I'll have a shot and a beer. Blackberry brandy and a draft are fine," Richard says to the barmaid.

The barmaid looks for money first, not caring about the patron's condition.

Richard downs his drinks. He's past a state of self-control.

"Here I go again, I'm all boozed up," Richard says softly.

"I better get out of here before my mind starts going weird."

Richard couldn't quite contain his interest in the gal next to him. She's a queen to Richard as his common sense flew the coop. She's puffing on a cigarette and her ample figure is busting out of her blouse. Richard starts talking to the girl, who is one step away from inebriation.

"You and I have a lot in common, baby," Richard says. His macho style is all dictated by the booze.

"I'm solving the problems in the Middle East. Here's one of my classic solutions. Why don't the Jews just move to a safer place? The terrorists are just going to keep killing. They come here with hatred and try to burn our nation with terror attacks."

Richard didn't have a chance to finish his lecture. Richard's new friend fell off her bar stool. Richard did his best to catch her. The party girl and questionable beauty queen brushed herself off. She had no shame and laughed off the bozo fall. That act did it. Richard decides he better get out of there before he ends up the same way.

The walk home is uneventful. He crosses five streets. Two skunks pass by along the way. He makes it home and uses the bathroom as a finish to an evening out. He lies on the bedroom bed and closes his eyes. His mind enters a drunken sleep. He dreams.

"How did I get here? This house, I worked here once. The Fairport Harbor beach is full of bathers. In clear sight is the breakwall. The water is rippling from the breeze. Is the Marti Gras here again?"

"What's out there? The terrorists are on the lake and they're going to do the unthinkable. They have weapons drawn. Mortars tubes on board the boats are being loaded. It's a nightmare. Is this happening again?"

Richard, quite intoxicated, watches as the room spins. He's semi-conscious watching this illusion. This nightmare is vivid and in color. His shot and beer drinking wake up the nemesis. His dreams are back to haunt him.

He raises his binoculars, firmly pressing them against his eyes.

"I see the two enemy yachts positioning themselves. The men on board are loading their mortars. They have the terrorist flags flying above the yachts. I remember that lion symbol. It's the terrorists again. It looks like one man has a shoulder fired RPG launcher."

"What's happening? Is it the booze again," asks Richard?

Richard looks at the clock next to the bed.

"It's four in the morning," he says.

Richard is still reeling from the night at the bar. His blood shot eyes strained to see in the darkness. His head flops back on the pillow. He can't stay awake. Almost immediately, his dream starts again.

Richard screams, "The people on the boats are terrorists."

"Get out of the water, everyone, get out of the water."

"They can't hear me, why? You knuckle head, open the window," Richard scolds himself.

He struggled to lift open the pane of glass and yell to the bathers. The house sits about two hundred yards from the sand bar near the lake. Richard is about seventy-five yards from the edge of the road next to the parking lot. He's so close to the fight.

"Take cover, take cover." He's screaming at the people on the beach.

"The terrorist are attacking. Run for cover."

What appears through a blue haze in the sky is the image of an Erie Indian. He is overlooking the battle scene. What takes place next is a scene from the War of 1812. A tall ship, the Lawrence, comes out of the harbor. It rounds the Fairport Harbor federal pier. The ship is setting its main sails. All of a sudden, puff. The sails fill with wind. The Lawrence is at full sail, picking up speed. She has aligned herself for an offensive attack.

Richard could see the captain.

"It's Commodore Perry on the tall ship. It is the flagship Lawrence. Commodore Perry is barking out the orders to the gun crew to let loose a broadside," Richard mumbles in disbelief.

Richard is wiping his eyes half crying. A discharge of cannon fire erupts from the Lawrence. It is directed at the first terrorist yacht. A pillar of black smoke fumes from the man of war. The thirty plus cannon fire is nearly on target. Richard can almost smell the acrid gun powder burning. The cannon balls are racking the water around the closest yacht. The water makes a geyser and puckers. Cannonballs pummel the yacht. The craft is badly damaged from the first salvos. It is hit forward and then aft. The terrorists on board cry out to each other. A small fire is started on the deck. One man was blown apart as he intercepted a cannonball. It hit him in the strike zone. He is dissected in front of fellow terrorists as the crew tries to regain control of the craft. They are stunned.

The commander of the second yacht is shocked. He decides he has seen enough of their sister yacht. His engine lights up in a roar. The escape route to the east is his only choice.

Richard is amazed by the speed of the Lawrence. He thought for a second.

"Commodore Perry is going to bring his ship to bear on the second yacht," he whispers.

Commodore Perry can't keep up with the motorized yacht but the sailors from the past saved the day. The bathers on the beach are running and cheering for the buccaneers. This fight isn't over yet.

To Richard's amazement another vessel appears. It's a swift boat. This Viet Nam vintage craft is after the second yacht. This speedster is running full speed ahead. The commanding officer is having his forward gun mount readied. He barks an order to the gunner. Richard can almost hear him say, 'Hold your fire, mate.'

They close rank and then take defensive action to prevent the terrorist from getting a fix on their position. The escaping terrorists are struggling to hold their balance as their yacht bounces along the water. A terrorist fires an RPG projectile. It explodes well off the mark. The swift boat decides to follow at a safe distance. They take evasive action by turning sharply. First, the navy craft move toward the shore then it heads in the opposite direction. The terrorist believe they have escaped. This short lived notion is shattered by a missile from an aircraft closing from above their craft. The ensuing volcanic blast breaks the yacht into two pieces. The attacking F-15 fighter finishes the job with a swooping dive. A close inspection of the remains eliminates any question about the damage. The terrorists on board are finished.

"You can go terrorize the devil," Richard screams.

A second F-15 buzzes the area to verify a successful mission.

Richard opens his eyes. He can smell gun powder. His gun cabinet is next to the bed and the door is open.

An old .38 caliber revolver sits just inside the cabinet door. It was a gun Richard was afraid to fire. He bought it years ago from a drunken man needing beer money.

"Could it be that nothing has happened? Was it all a dream? I can't tell anyone about this. Did I somehow lose contact with the world? Was I hallucinating?

I may end up in the mental hospital if the blackouts start happening again. I better stop drinking."

Richard opens the door and immediately senses the same acrid smell in the dream. It could be a passer-by just lit a cigarette. The morning newspaper is lying on the ground. The Lake County Voice brings Richard back to reality. He picks it up and returns to the kitchen table. He sets the paper down and starts a pot of coffee.

The morning routine is interrupted by nature so Richard visits the bathroom. The coffee maker is doing its usual puff and sputter. He grabs his favorite coffee cup. It is the cup with old glory painted on the side. He reaches the coffee maker and pours a hot one. He grabs the International Creamer from the refrigerator and adds one sugar. The alcoholic is getting a sugar fix to steady his vibrating body. His friend, Dave, a recovering alcoholic, told him about adding maple syrup to help the body calm the shakes. Richard doesn't need a fix like that right now. He figures he'll be OK until noon. Then he can down a cold one.

He opens the paper to the headlines: TERRORISTS MISS OPPORTUNITY TO INVADE FAIRPORT HARBOR. After a week of investigations, the FBI has concluded the terrorists were here for about two years. They used stores and a Canadian marina to plan a deadly attack. Richard revisits his worst nightmare. He can't stomach the coffee. He reads down the subtitle. It says the ATTACK WOULD HAVE STARTED IN MENTOR HEADLANDS. Interrogators found out parts of the plan from prisoners. The terrorists have gained a foothold into Middle America. Some of the terrorists were left to fend for themselves.

All of these developments make Richard feel a little edgy.

He jumps to his feet and runs to the bathroom. He looks in the mirror. He can't face the fact that America is under attack.

"One of the things we need to do is get off the foreign oil. Stop giving those bastards our money."

He decides to head for the basement to get his survival equipment. He knows he's got a six pack of beer stashed away for emergency purposes.

"Well, this is an emergency," Richard says to himself. He pops a tab off a 16 ounce tall boy. It's 9:30am. What a way to start the weekend.

He looks at the newspaper again and sees the date on the paper.

"This is a July newspaper."

Someone put an old newspaper in front of his house.

Richard fires up his HP computer.

"I'm going to start writing these visions down."

As he chokes down the first beer, he sees the vision of the Erie Indian again. He's still under the effects of last nights drinking. His mind starts to hallucinate.

The Erie Indian has a lion on a leash.

"What's this mean, an animal under control? Are the terrorist simply animals who haven't been tamed?"

"Dear God, I know you have picked on me to help do your work. I'm under the influence again and I'm having a tough time understanding. What is your message? Couldn't you find a college grad? Why me, God?" asks Richard.

As Richard finishes the first beer, he's overcome with another vision. His vision comes along in quick flashes. He is hallucinating.

Richard sees a car chase taking place near the border in Texas. An ATF officer and the Texas highway patrol are in pursuit of a BMW with Ohio license plates. The images come at him one after another. A Texas judge grabs his gavel and slams it down. He sees the shackled prisoner let away. First one prisoner, two more, and then he watches the prisoners load into a plane. Once inside the airplane and airborne, a big man pushes a guy out the cargo hatch.

He snaps out of the hallucination

"The big man isn't wearing prison clothes."

Richard continues to type away recording his hallucination as if copying pieces of history. His water logged brain sends messages to his fingers as he types on the computer. He's typing away as if possessed. Sometimes, he catches a fine detail.

A sign, *"El Paso, this is the Rio Grande."*

"I saw that. God is telling me to watch for these pictures."

Another beer later, *Richard sees a plane flying from a desert airstrip. Below the plane, a river is shown.*

"Is this area in south Texas? Am I witnessing some kind of operation going on near Mexico? This is Mexico," Richard answers himself.

The Mexicans are being loaded into a military truck. Could this be the Mexican Army? They converge on an airplane. Soon a cargo truck pulls up with two escort cars. The persons inside the cars look like terrorists. With that, a shootout takes place as the plane taxi's away from the action. It's a stalemate as each warring group retreats.

"Maybe, the Mexican army was trying to stop the terrorist," He wonders.

A sign proclaims in a newspaper clipping, 'Spain expels a Moroccan diplomat. The French have broken a terrorist cell.'

He sees a fire at a mosque and it looks to him like the place is surrounded by French police. Several bodies lay in front of the place of worship.

"Are the French standing up and putting down this religious malaise?"

Richard is too drunk to continue as the third beer overwhelms him. He stops at this point and relieves himself. He goes straight for the bedroom. His head hits the pillow and he's out again. His sleep is disrupted by a momentary dream.

He can see a gun shop. He is in the store and buys a hand gun.

2

Remembering

The fire department responded to the North Perry vehicle fire. The 911 call, reported by a resident farmer, explained the situation.

"Fire, fire, you have an explosion and fire in a police car and pickup truck! Take Center Street to Lockwood Drive, turn right and go east! This is a North Perry farmer!

"Who are you sir?" asked the central dispatcher.

"This is God! Godfrey Ackman, I have to go!"

The call ended abruptly. Central Dispatch immediately sent police and fire to the area. A police car was involved, which prompted greater scrutiny. The grisly scene was roped off and deputy sheriffs were posted to protect the suspected crime scene. Roadblocks were set up to keep traffic well away from the charred remains. The August sun was about to set. Ominously looking over the scene was a scarecrow standing tall in the corn stalks. This smiling faced figure marked the spot of the crime. His body cast a shadow over the smoldering remains.

The first safety forces that arrive are deputy sheriff Rex Buckey and his partner, Sergeant Dave Gooden. The two veteran officers have military experience on their side. Both officers had served in the Army during the battle for Kuwait. The Gulf War experience came in handy as they studied the fatalities.

"This was no accident," says the sergeant.

"I had a bad feeling about the call from dispatch," Rex says to Sergeant Gooden.

The coroner pulls up in his car. He can see the obvious.

"Hello, Doc. We called dispatch. Then we heard dispatch call you. You can see body parts are missing from the victims. We have four fatalities that we can see so far. Rex circles around the area to make sure there aren't anymore casualties lying in the corn field. It's pretty obvious an explosive devise was used here," comments the sergeant.

"The newspapers said you guys rounded up all the terrorists. Is this what we have here? Do we have more terrorists in Lake County," asks the doctor?

Dr. Lee and his partner snap a few pictures of the scene. The doctor's eyes start to visualize the circumstances.

Sergeant Gooden is quick to say what has been bothering him.

"The doc knows. We still have terrorists in the county." The sergeant's words grab the attention of the coroner.

Dr. Lee examines a legless body of a female a few feet from the truck. Dr. Lee and his partner take close-up photos of the corpse and measure limbs to link the limb to the victim.

"I know what the sheriff is going to say. He'll say, 'Keep a lid on this. We don't need to stoke a community panic,'" says the sergeant.

"I thought we rounded up all these bastards. We'll let the sheriff know we have more work to do. You look around, Rex; someone might have crawled into the bushes."

"Wait till the news people get a taste of this, Dave."

"Christ, Rex, don't say taste right now. My stomach is churning."

Sergeant Gooden is hunched over ready to vomit. His last coffee and bagel are leaving him a little squeamish.

Teaming together, they know all too well what they have examined; scattered body parts, obviously ripped apart by a bomb in the pickup truck. The odor of C5 dynamite is still in the air.

"These women," Sergeant Gooden explains, "They aren't in North Perry, Ohio to pick apples. The armory of weapons they were carrying suggests one thing. Terrorists! They are here, Rex. We didn't get them all. The terrorist roundup will need to continue. Sheriff Clay is not going to be a happy camper. I'll try to think of some other reason for what I see."

"It's plain to me, sarge. What I see are radical Islamists. Someone sent these girls to the moon with a boom. Did they do it to themselves?" asks Rex.

Rex is unfazed by the carnage. He retains a sense of humor and muses with rhyming words.

"Who else would be carrying around a mortar?" asked the Sergeant.

The peace officer's car parked behind the wrecked truck withstood the blast. It turned out to be his last traffic stop. The officer was dead and slumped over the front seat.

"Dave, this is the second time in the last couple months we've been called to check out explosives, only this time someone is using the stuff. A bad element is in our county. A nasty group has dynamite and they aren't afraid to use it. The military had a chance to stop these terrorists in Iraq and Iran. What did the Republicans do? What did the Democrats do? Don't answer! We had a chance to topple Saddam Hussein when we were there with General Schwarzkopf. Do you remember the famous 'left hook' maneuver, Dave? The United Nations messed that up. Now, we have Congress ready to cut and run. It's no wonder these terrorists are coming across our border. Is it ok for the terrorists to say this is a holy war. Why is there such a double standard in America?"

The smoldering wreck was clearly a case for the FBI. Two agents were immediately dispatched to investigate. FBI Agent Ron Roman and Bill Wright arrive from Cleveland to examine the remains.

"It looks like the women became victims themselves. This was no accident. I'm not in any hurry to make a snap decision on this case but." Agent Roman stops in midstream with his explanation. His mind reflects on the past.

Not long ago Agents Roman and Wright received orders to investigate a shady Grand River development project. Village officials in Lake County were thought to be involved. In doing that, they uncovered sketchy details of a terrorist cell. A plan to attack somewhere in Lake County, presumably the Perry Nuclear Power Plant, was suspected. Certainly, the nuclear plant was considered most likely. The agents used a combination of investigational methods to crack the case wide open. A river stakeout, telephone taps, and tips from citizens provided the crime fighters with a picture of the criminals and their likely target. The two men brought in a dragnet of lawmen. They stopped a terrorist organization from unleashing a murderous attack on the village of Fairport Harbor.

The FBI agents constructed a picture of the three women killed in the explosion. They were adults. Their ages probably ranged from the late twenties to near forty. They carried an arsenal of weaponry. Pistols, machine guns, hand grenades, and even a mortar were found in the truck. An interesting piece of evidence was recovered in the field nearby. It proved to be especially useful. One of the three females must have carried a diary. The fresh diary entry said the women lived in Painesville. They had apparently fled from a Painesville safe house.

A police officer in a patrol car that initially approached the women from behind met a violent fate. The dead officer at the scene made an attempt to stop the female terrorists. He was killed by the blast from a hand grenade after initially being wounded by gunshots. Two of the occupants in the truck were blown out the side doors while the third victim was projected skyward finally coming to rest on the side of the road. She was apparently riding in the back of the truck bed.

The two detectives finished up their initial investigation. The deputy sheriffs and the G-men exchanged handshakes.

"The terrorist case is open again. You can tell your boss that," says Agent Roman to Sergeant Gooden.

"Oh, he'll want to hear that," sighs Sergeant Gooden.

The two G-men returned to Cleveland to study the evidence they collected.

One of the dead women, who carried the diary, detailed her journey to America on a freighter called the *Gupka*. Agent Wright found a note folded away in the diary case.

The note said, *Phase two, Nigerian Embassy has Mahdi's plan for DC.*

The diary mentioned, Omma and a twin sister, Olga. It went on to say, *we made the journey with the other stowaways on the Gupka.* This passage caused a red flag to be raised as other terrorists might still be in the country. The diary provided insight into the gestation of a terrorist cell. Clearly, a good amount of planning was needed to bring these women to America. The reach of al Qaeda was surrounding the globe. The agents checked with the coast guard in order to find the freighter, *Gupka*. The freighter, *Gupka,* is in the Atlantic Ocean heading back to Turkey.

"How many of these terrorists reside in America?" Agent Wright wondered aloud.

Agent Roman and Wright gather facts on cases along the northern border across the United States. They are assigned to lead investigations involving terrorist activity. Washington, Oregon, Michigan, Ohio, and New York, report activities related to al Qaeda. Canada is being used as a conduit to enter America.

Agent Roman and Wright shuttled among the northern states where terrorist activity was suspected. They assembled a terrorist file in these states. Dating the occurrence, the agents developed a timeline. The progression of reports is growing. The threat to national security is increasing.

The two investigators become engrossed in their work. Protecting America from the radical Islamic menace is a top priority in their lives. They manage to mix business with pleasure much to the chagrin of Supervisor Cliff Moses.

Roman starts to experiment with infrared signaling and detection equipment. He bugs his German shepherd, named Pin-um. Ron tracks Pin-um using radio frequency equipment. He attaches the device to the dog's collar and drops the dog off at Bill Wright's house. Using a laptop computer, a signal illuminates a dot on the screen. It is amazingly accurate.

"We have to show this to Agent Monica and Paula," said Agent Wright.

"OK Romeo. Will you ever give up on those two," asked Agent Roman?

"No way, Ron, you know me."

The men give the two female agents a lesson in tracking using Pin-um as the simulated terrorist. The female agents, who work in the same department, are impressed. They ask Agent Bill Wright to program one for them. Agent Wright, who is always trying to score points with the girls, makes sure that they are the second team to have one. He programs it and he brings it over himself.

"This is portable. You can use it anywhere. Just don't tell Cliff. He doesn't have to know about this," said Agent Wright.

The device worked well on the dog. Agent Roman and Wright were confident that the bug would come in handy someday.

They devise a plan to track terrorist suspects. Without telling Supervisor Cliff Moses, they plan to bug individuals they suspect as being al Qaeda members. Their mutual feeling is the enemy puppets would lead them to the hands of the manipulator. The legality issues would have to be worked out. The device would help them in their quest to nab the enemy. They believe a day would come when they will have an opportunity to try out the tracking device.

"The ringleader is out there, Bill. We have a new tool in our crime fighting arsenal. If we ever get the chance to use this, we better make darn sure a judge has given the OK."

Agent Roman holds the small electronic chip between his index finger and thumb.

"We are lawmen, Bill. You know we wouldn't do anything illegal. No, not us. Cliff would do a back flip if we don't go through legal channels. Do you think we would ever do something illegal?"

3

Used Cars in West Virginia

The terrorists that enter Ohio from Canada deploy to ever expanding areas. Cell members are encouraged to set up shops on a line, much like a vein in the body. Lake Erie is the heart pumping fresh terrorist recruits south into Northern Ohio and Buffalo, New York.

The night of hallucinations and nightmares is a call to Richard. He should see a doctor. He paces the house as if he is in a cage. Withdrawing from the effects of the booze is difficult for him. He eases the pain by drinking an eye-opener. The beer reduces his anxiety. By noon he is somewhat better but jittery. He refreshes himself with a shower and leaves his house knowing full well he is struggling with addiction. He heads to a tavern hoping to establish the stabilizing level of alcohol he needs. At the bar in Painesville, it didn't take him long to visualize the enemy.

He experiences a vision that appears as a reflection on the bay window of the tavern. The reflection is shaped like a map of Lake Erie. Dots are illuminated on the map. Richard thought to himself in that fleeting moment that these are terrorist bases. Streaks of light emanating from the dots portray a terrorist departure from the base on the north side of Lake Erie. The fading light melts away to be followed by another. They all vanish in a drop as if gravity drives the direction.

Across the street, lights illuminate the wide red brick road in front of this tavern. A neon sign flickers on and off into the empty street. Further down the street, Richard could see the run down train depot and a train whizzing across the tracks behind it. The train is carrying automobiles. The train conductor unleashes a bull horn message. It is not stopping at the railroad crossing ahead. The thumping wheels of the train and the flickering sign act like a psychiatrist's watch in front of his face. He is hypnotized. A terrorist thought pops into his head at the same time.

Richard could see a string of automobiles carried on the train cars. The terrorists are somehow tied to this mode of transportation. They are involved with moving autos.

Richard grasped the importance of this thought. This is a method the terrorists use to distribute their people. Nonchalantly, he whispers his inner notion to an uncaring fellow seated next to him.

"The terrorists are moving," Richard says. The wisdom of his sentence bypasses the stranger. The stranger's eyes are glassy, as if to say he is fully loaded. Richard may as well talk to his beer mug. Richard pipes a little louder.

"The terrorists are moving again. We didn't eliminate all of them from this area." His frankness caught the ear of the bartender. Bob, the bartender, retorts.

"You know something, Richard? You are starting to become an authority around here. I'm hearing it was you that tipped the FBI about the terrorists coming into the county."

The bartender was right. Richard did tip the FBI. His visit to the FBI headquarters in Cleveland to report a hunch about terrorists didn't fall on deaf ears. An agent, named Ron Roman, logged his statement.

No reward money was earned with this tip. Richard's drinking habit was partly responsible for that. The agent couldn't ignore the odor of beer testing his senses. Richard offered his candor about terrorists coming from Canada. Agent Roman's first thought was to stick this hunch in the circular file, but he didn't. He chose to notate for future reference.

"You want to know something, Bob; I'm going to make some serious money. You gave me an idea. I'm going to start another business," says Richard. Without elaborating, Richard downs the beer and leaves.

Richard pulls into his driveway. He walks into the house and picks up a pen. The thought he has is a brilliant idea. He must write it down. Only two words need to be written. The underscore adds importance.

BOUNTY HUNTER

He lies down and is asleep rather quickly. A dream appeared during his alcohol induced sleep. It is during the dream he could see himself.

Richard is sitting down at a desk in a fancy motel room. The spacious room with a high ceiling is a departure from the standard motel.

He's writing a note to FBI Agent Ron Roman. The note is detailed.

The terrorists are dispersing, moving by train, in cars, and they have small boats. I saw the boats that were used for the foiled Fairport Harbor operation. These boats are small, sixteen or eighteen foot types. The water borne terrorists are able to conceal their identity by imitating fishermen. Overland they make use of used car dealerships. These auto pawn shops are mobile stations that can be used by terrorists to conceal a vehicle or exchange it.

The terrorist leaders have look-alike members filling in for them. The mayors of Fairport Harbor and Grand River never realized they were dealing with substitutes. Nearly all of the leadership remains on the loose. The police have arrested shadows. The real leadership is still out there.

I saw a terrorist cell containing two young members. This duo was anxious to set up a used car dealership south of the Ohio River. They had ten used cars loaded on a truck trailer. They picked a quiet town in West Virginia. I saw a sign. On it was, Welcome to Parkersburg.

The next morning Richard calls the FBI Cleveland headquarters and speaks to Agent Ron Roman. He knew Richard very well. Agent Roman's previous experience in dealing with terrorism and Richard's insight into terrorism gave him some clout when talking to the FBI. Richard used this clout to reach Agent Roman.

"Hello Ron, this is Richard Stern."

"What's up Mr. Stern? Did you have another revelation?"

"Ron, you better sit down if you aren't already. I am going to deliver terrorists schemes to you that may be hard for you to swallow. The authorities have the wrong people in jail. Oh, they might be terrorists. They are not the leaders. On top of that, the terrorists are moving inland."

"I remember seeing a sign along the highway, Ron. It said, 'Welcome to Parkersburg, West Virginia. Take the next two exits.' It was something like that. Hey, it's a dream. How do we remember every detail in a dream? That is the million dollar question. Don't worry; the FBI can just fork over a wad of Ulysses Grants. That will be enough this time. As the dreams become more definitive, the reward money should be more definitive. I was rather excited about the clarity of the dream. The sign will lead you to more terrorists. I'm sure of it. They are moving down south," says Richard.

He adds more. "I don't know how this dream unfolds."

"I was sitting in a tavern last night and a train went through Painesville loaded with cars. That picture set something off in me."

"It couldn't have been the booze," injects Agent Ron.

"Very funny, Ron, I'm serious. You guys better check this out. Put some reward money aside for me," adds Richard.

"Agent Ron, I wrote this crazy note last night. How many used car dealerships could there be in Parkersburg? Why did I have this dream of terrorists?"

"There is one other thing Ron, I'm going to learn about bounty hunting."

The phone goes dead for a few seconds.

"Ron, are you there?"

Agent Ron almost dropped the phone when Richard said he would learn about bounty hunting. He gathered his composure.

"You leave investigating to us, Mr. Stern. We need you for your criminal tracking instincts."

Richard wanted to secure any reward money that the FBI had to offer. After all, he was supplying them with valuable information. He felt the least they can do is grease the tracks of their informer.

"My criminal tracking instincts don't pay like a bounty hunter's work does."

"We will check out this story, Richard. The FBI will keep you in mind for reward money if we make a connection with your lead. You better be careful about driving in your condition. You might want to see your doctor again. I would hate to see you end up in the detox again. You should try a Coke or a Pepsi once in a while. One of these days, you are going to end up with some bar fly. Of course, that might be a good thing for you."

Agent Roman was half joking and continued.

"You give us a call if you see more. In the meantime, Bill Wright and I will have a look around Parkersburg, West Virginia."

Agent Roman hangs up the phone and pages Agent Wright. While waiting for a call back he reaches into his desk for a map of America. He leafs through the pages until he comes to West Virginia.

Bill Wright calls back within minutes.

"Bill, listen up. I have another dual trip lining up for us. We are heading for West Virginia.

"Interstate 77 runs through Parkersburg, West Virginia. Richard Stern just had another vision and he claims a potential terrorist cell is setting up there. We better check it out. It's a used car business, he says. This potential drop off point would enable terrorists to change cars. I think the terrorists are trying to exchange their getaway cars. They are masking their means of transportation."

"Stern was out drinking again so we better be prepared. This could be a hot tip. Something else is a potential problem. Somebody better watch Mr. Stern. I think he wants to be a bounty hunter."

"What," asks Agent Wright?

"Yeah, he said something like that. He wants reward money."

"We better have a special detail keep a watch on him. He might be hitting the bottle hard again and we need to protect our tipster. See if you can line up a cover to track him."

"I'll call Monica and Paula and see who's available," says Agent Bill.

"Bill, I've always wanted to fish the streams in West Virginia."

"You and I will be taking on the hillbilly terrorists. We want to be observers first. So our cover will be this fishing trip. As a side bar to our terrorist hunting, a fishing trip to West Virginia is definitely in order. Let's hope Richard Stern dreams contain a few rainbow trout for us."

"You know, Ron, if he starts looking into the bounty hunting business, he just might put us out of work."

"Listen Bill, that guy has enough problems without chasing terrorists."

4

The Flight of Mr. Big

The next layer of terrorism has already taken shape. Cell members have attended flight school in Texas. They have been taught about piloting small aircraft. They will be told to work for a small parcel carrier. This small carrier business has leased and purchased planes to service special markets where people, money, and drugs will be exchanged.

Captain Awad is organizing a new cell. His leader, Mr. Big, has approved new plans to create panic in Washington, DC. Mr. Big is a ruthless killer of anyone that steps in his way. He kills his own members if they make the slightest slipup. He runs the North American al Qaeda organization. His use of shadows or look-a-like members to escape from capture has kept him free. He has connections in New York, Washington DC and mosques across North America. His tall stature is a problem for him. A man over six feet five inches is a noticeable individual in a crowd. Captain Awad is a slippery right hand man. The captain has earned a notorious reputation for concocting vicious attacks in Europe, Asia, and Africa. He has been brought to North America to coordinate multiple terrorist attacks. Mr. Big and Captain Awad form the third cell in America. Through their plans, a new terrorist group emerges to foster crime against the West.

Al Qaeda has learned some lessons that have cost it many soldiers. The West is too strong militarily. They can't take on the American military in a direct fight for sure. The Tora Bora disaster in Afghanistan was a brutal lesson. Mr. Big and Osama Bin Laden narrowly escape that fiasco. City fighting in Iraq was taking down important soldiers of al Qaeda. Captain Awad withdrew from Fallujah, Iraq after losing many soldiers. He evacuated to the city of Mosul. Later, he fought at the Syrian border with American troops. When the insurgent captain lost soldiers that were earmarked for the American campaign, he was pulled from Iraq. Captain Awad was able to use Canada as a staging ground for planned attacks in Middle America.

The West's successful operations around the world invigorated another batch of secret lawmen. America and other aligned nations have rebuilt an undercover police corps called Interpol, an anti-terrorism, anti-crime network. These men and women are chasing down the terrorists before they can develop dastardly deeds. Interpol police have developed a fast tracking system. Terrorist suspects are recorded in a data base. This terrorist list is distributed to nations supporting Interpol. The enforcement group is emerging as an effective weapon to counter the terrorists. They have taken out many cell members. Some cells have relocated to safer nations. Other terrorist cells are moving about disbanded. It is as if they are a rack of balls on a pool table. The rolling white knight of Interpol slams into a lead cell and the balls of terrorism shift around the world's table. Some cell members disappear by the hands of Interpol police, never to be heard from again.

The terrorists must mutate. They hide. Eventually, some are hunted down. Do or die service is taught to terrorist members. To often the die aspect of terrorism is the end. This code of conduct keeps many members from falling into the hands of Interpol. Suicide bombers don't make it to America.

Inside the safety of a Washington, DC embassy, Al Qaeda leadership tells Mr. Big to hurry along with more stateside attacks. Mr. Big plans with Captain Awad even though recruiting members are drying up. This further strains Mr. Big's American plan.

In a couple of American cities, the terrorists take secure routes to safe houses using their new incubating air service. This system of using private planes is working. The disguise of an air and parcel taxi service helps relocate cell members. When the heat is on, a cell takes flight to another location using this service. A shell game goes into effect if the FBI lawmen close in.

Bogus records of passengers are kept on file. Used cars shuttle cell members across state lines. This used car business is a handy service. It enables terrorists to mobilize and escape across borders. A cell member that is being hounded merely moves to another city and relocates to a friendly food store or a safe house. This method is saving members from being caught. By using small airplanes and used cars, the harried cell member can escape the dragnet in America. The small airline company is called Lion Air. It is another legitimate company similar to the food stores and a couple of marinas operating in select cities. The used car business is becoming a very attractive way to hide cell members. The US auto industry is facing a glut in used cars. Because of this, used car lots are filled with worthy transportation to move the terrorists.

The connection in El Paso to Cindad Juarez, Mexico has worked well for the last two years. Recently though, it has come to the terrorist leadership's attention that El Paso's used car dealership is wavering.

The recent terrorist bust in Ohio was the start of a new frontal assault on terrorism. Ohio became a focus state because the terrorists were able to infiltrate into the state with enough forces. FBI agents were on guard after they found a terrorist air strip and new safe house in a Pennsylvania mountain.

Ohio terrorist cell members found a way to escape. They had to melt into the country. The terrorists moved their team using a small aircraft, a used car and a local freight train. An escape from the Pennsylvania mountain camp using several transportation modes made it tough to track the cell members. The small base camp where they made an airfield was used effectively. Some members made the exit to Mexico. From there, they traveled to the next hideout. Other members had a bad ending. The ones who elected to travel with Mr. Big became martyrs. Mr. Big made his way back to a safe mosque in Germany. Mr. Big made a tough decision. As unsavory as this was, he must keep his role secret from the other cell members.

From a Pennsylvania camp, individual cell members were told to pair up and work their way to El Paso, Texas. Once there, they would be supplied help to make their exit from society until the next orders arrived. One set of members boarded a train going south. They hitchhiked a ride on a slow train for a night ride. As the train was coming to a stop, they jumped to safety. They kidnapped a motel worker and her car for the final leg of their journey. The lady's body was dumped off in a forested area in Alabama. These two terrorists showed up at a safe store, Max Renolds's store. Max didn't waste any time with these two after reading the headlines about the Ohio terror attack. He sent them away by virtue of a ride to the Mexican border. A small fee was paid to the Mexican authorities to transport the two farther South. They would eventually reach Mexico City. They could wait it out there before returning.

Two terrorists weren't so lucky. They were riding with Mr. Big in a plane headed toward Texas. At least that is what they were told. Along the route, celebratory ice tea was served to the terrorists. The contents of the drinks were spiced with a very relaxing potion. Somewhere along the ride an accident occurred. The two men fell from the plane at three thousand feet.

"They really should have been strapped in. They got careless by the open bay door. A nasty turbulence caused the two to take a plunge." Mr. Big would recall.

Mr. Big did not like to take a chance with some people. If he wasn't totally sure they could keep their mouth closed, he removed the subject. The planes destination ended in remote Mexico. Mr. Big traveled to Cancun and flew to Brazil. The Gupka, a Turkish freighter, picked him up for a ride to France.

A third cell got into a shoot-out with the FBI in Louisville, Kentucky. Their car ride was intercepted by the West Virginia Highway Patrol. The FBI had a description of the car that was seen leaving the camp in Pennsylvania. This car matched that car. The FBI asked the highway patrol to let them go without raising a suspicion. The West Virginia H. P. made a brilliant maneuver to out wit the terrorists. After confirming that the car they were monitoring was indeed a possible Ohio attacker, and the center of attention, they passed the car with flasher lights lit and pulled over a dummy car. The terrorists were fooled into thinking the patrol was after a speeder. The terrorists were monitored from above using a tracking aircraft. The FBI decided to see where they were going. The terrorists stopped at a motel in Louisville. Orders to the local FBI came quickly. Move in; take them down before other citizens get mixed up with these two. The motel was half filled and the FBI made an attempt to seize them without trouble. A full fledged fire fight erupted. The two terrorists fell dead in a hail of automatic bullets fired by both FBI agents and SWAT. Later, while inspecting the get-a-way car a major find was uncovered. The terrorists had bomb vests stored in the trunk of the getaway car. They just didn't have time to dress.

5

The Bounty Hunter

Richard Stern slowly cut down on his drinking. After two weeks, he was feeling good about himself. He was on a path toward recovery. He eventually quit drinking altogether and attended a few AA meetings as Father Pete suggested. Unfortunately, his recovery would not last. He believes he can control his drinking this time.

Richard decides to try a self styled vigilantism. He is going to find the terrorists using his special power. His use of alcohol would help him find the terrorists. Richard will scout around the country and deal with these bad guys. Richard isn't satisfied with just helping the FBI with terrorist tips by way of his dreams. His dreams could become a ticket to riches. He will follow his mystical inspirations and hunt down the bad guys. God gave him a power to see what is going to happen. The booze just activates this power.

"I'm a pawn for the FBI but the information gathered about the terrorists should pay a bounty. The FBI will get informational tips and the FBI can pay rewards back. The FBI might supply tidy rewards for this detective work."

To start his new occupation, he decides to examine past steps taken by the terrorists. He records known information about terrorists. The Canada to Ohio connection was covered by the media. Some terrorists were apprehended in Buffalo, New York. Buffalo would be his starting point. He will follow his dreams. Maybe he can pick up their trail.

He had several leads on where the terrorists were. According to the Lake County Voice, the local newspaper, the escape route had terrorists going to Buffalo, New York. From there, they were sighted in Pennsylvania. A mountain camp in PA was used as a hideout.

"I'm going to take a ride up to New York first. I'll visit that used car dealership, called the Lemon Tree, where the terrorist had rented cars. Maybe I can pick up a clue." He read about bounty hunting. He used the local library in Fairport Harbor to gather details of past terrorist operations from old literature. He read books, magazines and newspaper clippings about terrorist activity. He found the names of fugitives and the bounty that could be collected if the information was used to nab these criminals.

According to an FBI report between five and ten terrorists from Ohio are still on the run. Police had arrested eleven so far. Three food stores were shutdown and two safe houses were boarded up. Around three hundred thousand dollars was seized along with guns and bomb making material. Richard collected a good bit of information on what transpired before and after the terrorist ring was broken. There were several confrontations with terrorists along the border with Canada, so he knew terrorists were still trying to operate in America. The West Virginia highway patrol tracked a pair of terrorists. A confrontation followed and the bad guys were shot dead at a motel.

Richard had enough money to start his bounty business. He had been paid several fees from magazine articles he wrote. He also was paid for his amateur photo work. He got lucky at a bingo game and won eighteen hundred bucks last week. All this new wealth would supply him with seed money to make his first business trip. Dividend checks from an investment would cover his house payments and insurance over the next six months. He figured he had a nice tidy sum to start.

"What am I? I'm a bounty hunter," says an overly confident Richard Stern.

If Richard could land one of the terrorists, he could collect a fair reward.

"Fair, I'll be rich," he says.

Some of the fugitives had hefty rewards for their capture. Richard could make a pretty good living by snaring any one of these monsters. Several of them had over a hundred thousand dollars in rewards on their heads. Richard definitely had an incentive to help bring any one of these guys to justice.

"I'm starting a new business. *Richard's Bounty Business*," he thought.

He won't tell anyone about this idea because he'll get the same old negative line. "You're nothing but a drunk and a dreamer," people will say.

"I'm not going to let the booze beat me. The only person I'll confide in is Father Pete. I'll let him know what I'm doing. I'll take my camera and write a story along the way. I'll submit an article to the Reader's Digest. They pay for good stories. There are plenty of magazines that would beg a story from me if I could catch one of these dudes. I'm going to be in on the action. America, you are the land of opportunity. Dear God, don't hold me back. I'm going hunting," proclaims Richard.

Richard went through a firearms training program, so he could carry a concealed weapon. He missed the target a good portion of the time at the practice range. At least he didn't shoot himself in the foot. Because he was such a bad shot, he thought about leaving the gun at home. He ends up deciding to take a handgun with him just in case he ran into a problem. He just might need to shoot it out with the bad guys.

Richard bought a .22 Magnum revolver for protection It had room for eight bullets. The salesman at the gun store told him to buy hollow point shells. He took his advice. Richard never was a gun enthusiast so he didn't see a need for some huge hand gun that he couldn't handle. The salesman suggested he go with more stopping power.

"Mr. Stern, consider this deterrent. Here is a .38 Magnum," The salesman presented a good looking Smith and Wesson hand gun. It had a nice shiny look but Richard didn't agree.

"I'm on a budget. I'm not going to be shooting anyone," said Richard. He thought about what he said. Would he shoot at someone?

"With a camera, yes I would. With my magnum pistol, I don't know."

6

Bar and Bird

September is ending. The leaves are starting to fall from the trees. It's a nice day as Richard loads up his van. He studies a checklist of items that he should take on his first ever bounty mission. He marks the list as he calls out numerous items suit case, camera, laptop computer, toothbrush, cooler and finally at the end of the list, a map. Near the end of his list is the memo: Take the equalizer.

One of the last items on his list is the handgun. He must decide if he really needs a gun. It just seems like it would invite trouble if he has it. He remembers the instructor saying, "The bad guy is probably going to have a knife or a gun. Why not carry and be prepared to use an equalizer?" That makes sense to Richard so he goes back to the house to retrieve his equalizer.

The local gun dealer set him up. He has a shoulder holster that fits the gun nicely. They know how to dress a bounty hunter. The problem for Richard, he needs someone to help him shoot straight and the gun dealer only had a right-handed shoulder holster.

Richard walks into his bedroom and tries wearing his concealed weapon. He looks in the mirror to see just how menacing he appears. He draws the gun and points it at the mirror.

"This is just plain creepy. Elliot Ness is at your service. Holy cow, what am I doing? This just isn't me. I'm not a gun guy," says the doubting Richard.

He takes the holstered gun off and carries the equalizer to the van. He has a box of hollow point shells which he stuffs in a pocket inside the suitcase. The suitcase has a lock on it but he doesn't remember the combination. The lock is broke anyhow. He broke it the last time he used it. Richard puts the gun and holster next to the suitcase in an empty shoe box. He wraps a large rubber band around the box. This all seems too movie like for Richard.

Before he takes off in earnest, his final stop this Sunday morning is at St. Anthony's Church. He needs to see Father Pete and let him know that he is going away for a month or so. Father Pete has become a crutch for him to lean on when his personal weakness gets the best of him. In the back of Richard's mind is his waning will power. Father Pete knows what Richard will do. Richard's hands shake a little as if to remind him that his body is yearning for another drink.

He drives to St. Anthony's Church on Fifth and Vine. Richard wants to light a candle and make an offering before Mass. His mission is clear, but his motive is slightly tainted. Richard hasn't had a drink in a while but this mission could call for him to deviate from sobriety.

"Father Pete, I'm going to New York for a photo session and I'm going to be working on a magazine article. It's a shot in the dark type project. It might turn a couple bucks. Don't think I'm out boozing it up when I'm away." Richard's statement was the clearest sign of what's to come. Father Pete wishes Richard well and reminds him of his attraction to alcohol. Father Pete, a pillar, is steady and under control. He offers Richard sound advice.

"That stuff is your Achilles heel. Alcohol will point you in the wrong direction. You need to be a straight shooter." Father Pete says.

Richard realizes the implications of his words.

"Thanks Father, see you in November or early December. Some people refer to this job as a crusade. I call it a working vacation or missionary work."

Richard saw the look on Father Pete's face. He winced a little when Richard told him he's trying to do missionary work. Father Pete suspects that Richard is up to something more than a vacation. Richard remembers one of Father Pete's positive messages.

"You need God's help as you drive through life." Those are special words for Richard as he is about to hunt for the devils in America.

Richard drove down Ohio Rt. 2 until it turned into Rt.20. He drove by the towns of Perry, Madison, Geneva and Ashtabula. After an hour, he was almost to Conneaut, Ohio. He stopped at a BP gas station and topped off the fuel tank.

"This will get me into New York," said Richard, as he washed off the windshield.

He stops at a restaurant in Buffalo. He has a meat ball sandwich and a fountain Coke. While in the restaurant, he looks up the address of the used car lot that was used by the terrorists. Soon he is back in the van searching for the Lemon Tree used car lot.

His trip was going well as he cruised around not far from the city. In a small town called Blasdell, he found the Lemon Tree used car lot where the terrorists rented cars for their ride to the Pennsylvania mountain hideout. It was near the Lemon Tree that Richard decided to deviate. Richard saw a local tavern across the street from the used car lot and made the fateful decision.

"I'll have one." Deep down he wants to stay off the booze but the drive to find the terrorists told him otherwise. He could have a drink or two. Richard is determined to use all available methods to track down the bad guys. Is it an excuse to drink, he would ask himself? In all honesty, Richard was fighting the temptation to start drinking. His heart told him no alcohol. Father Pete said the same. He has to make a decision and that moment is upon him.

Once inside of Big Mike's Cafe, it is reminiscent of Richard's home town bar. A few exceptions are the piano in the corner and the small stage nearby. He fell in love with the atmosphere. Richard liked the fact that there aren't many customers in the bar. He surrenders to his weakness. Richard's willpower melts like a spring thaw. He quickly exchanges words with a young barmaid named Sandy.

"I see the sign says, 'Sandy on duty.' My name is Richard. I'm on a photo assignment and would like to take some pictures of the place." He said.

"I'm looking for terrorists."

Her eyes widened, as she watched him walk away.

"I'll tell you more after I get my camera." Richard didn't give her time to say no. He went out to his van and grabbed the digital camera. He had a connection with the barmaid so he went back in to pick her brain. It was five o'clock in the afternoon.

"I take pictures of crime scenes for magazines. The used car dealership across the street was involved in a crime. I understand terrorists were aided by vehicles rented from the used car business," he said.

The barmaid was sharp. She was dressed in jeans and had a shirt tucked in to reveal a model body. She was tall, blue eyed, blond and she probably played a mean forward in volleyball. She was in her early twenties. Her eyes lit up when Richard mentioned the used car dealership and terrorists.

The bar was situated at an angle to the used car lot. The barmaid could see the used car lot from the bay window.

"Do you remember seeing a bunch of police at the Lemon Tree a couple months back?" Richard asked.

"Do I remember?" Sandy asks.

"The cops were all over the place. Millie, the second shift relief, bought a car from the man who ran the business. We watched the cops move in. They put barrier tape across each entrance. Police dogs and the bomb squad were on the scene. Millie said the salesman and the owner were both arrested but I think just the owner was charged with a crime. The FBI came in here." Her eyes flashed as she explained in more detail.

"The used cars they sold or rented were used in a terrorist escape. I didn't see them take anyone away. After a day, they sealed off the whole lot and stayed there for three days. The place was closed for a month or more. It just reopened again a few weeks ago."

"Do you want anything to drink?" Sandy asks.

Richard hesitated. This was the defining moment. The barmaid, atmosphere, and booze were too much. Richard gave in.

"I'll have a draft," he said. Richard could feel the flood gates open. His weakness for booze was upon him. He took the step all alcoholics take.

Sandy walked over to the tap and poured a tall glass of beer as she talked.

"The man charged is a Syrian. He was leasing the property. This guy is part of a terrorist ring. That is the talk of the town. He is in jail, charged with conspiracy and aiding the enemy. We had four FBI agents in here. It was so cool."

Sandy was excited to talk about what happened. Richard could tell she told this story a dozen or more times.

"Two of the agents were from Buffalo and the other two were from Cleveland, Ohio."

"Do you remember their names; the FBI agents from Ohio?" Richard asked.

Sandy paused for a second and walked over to her purse. She reached into her purse and pulled out a business card.

"Agent Ron Roman, I have it here." She said.

"This business card is his. He was a giant. I mean, he was a big guy. He said call the FBI if I remembered anything that might help. Can you imagine all of this excitement?"

"I know Ron Roman. I did an interview with him in July. He is a big guy," said Richard.

"They interviewed both of us. Millie can talk more about it. She bought a car from the terrorist!"

"I don't think the owner drank. He never came in here. The cars he had on the lot were all impounded. The cars were in pretty nice shape. They weren't junks," said Sandy.

"Millie will be coming on duty at six o'clock. She'll give you an earful."

She continues, "Three or four big car trailers came by one day and picked up the cars. The terrorist had maybe thirty cars on the lot. I wish I could have got one."

"The new business owner, Tom Selby, stops in here every other day. He likes his beer. He brings his partner Bo LaJett with him. They reminisce about the high school days. They must have gone to the same school. They're not terrorists.

Tom wears a West Virginia tee shirt under his business suit and talks with a hill-billy accent. I like the guy. Bo is tall and quiet until he's had a few. He's a great talker as he fuels up with beer. He did a funny superman routine in here. He went into the men's room and changed into a costume of superman when he was loaded. I think he was previewing a stunt with Mr. Selby to gain popularity at their business. His audition was a riot."

Sandy knew quite a bit but Richard thought he better talk with Millie.

"Tom is always hitting on me but I don't date the clientele. He always leaves a nice tip after I get him drunk," she says.

"This babe is for me. Just get me a little drunk." Richard thought to himself.

He tried not to show his weakness for booze. His hands were shaking a little as he listened to her. He needed to have a couple more beers to calm down and he did.

"Sandy, I'm going to hang around for a while. I'd like to talk with Millie and get her take on the crime scene."

"She'll be here shortly." She says.

"Sandy, just think of me as a photographer/writer. I meet people for a living and need to dig into their business. I do independent writing for newspapers and magazines. I'm a little too nosey at times. You are a prime candidate for a terrorist article. I'm too old to be your boyfriend but would never turn down an offer if you want me to be your personal photographer."

Richard winked at her to let her know he is just trying to be friendly.

Sandy candidly replied, "I'm a very expensive model. Do you have a couple of mil?"

"Fix me up with another beer and a six pack to go. I'm going to walk over to the used car lot. I'd like to see what they have over there. I'll be back shortly."

Richard finished another brew and picked up his camera and a six pack. He snaps a picture of Sandy with her back to him. The light in the bar is low. He is not sure if the picture will turn out. He didn't want to activate the flash because that would change the casual mood.

He put the beer in his van and advanced on the car lot. The used car lot across the street was closed on Sunday. The owner had about twenty autos on the lot. Richard walks around a little, nosing near the driver's side windows of the cars. The cars are all locked. None of them had less then fifty thousand miles on the odometer. He snaps a few pictures and focuses on the business office. Richard could feel the beer working like magic. He only had a few beers but he hadn't had a drink in a few weeks. That layoff probably accounted for his quick buzz. He froze for a second and suddenly a thought ran into his head.

The Syrian owner had a silent partner who helped move the cars. They didn't get him. He's still somewhere close by.

As Richard stood on the sidewalk, he could feel the presence of someone watching him. He turned his head fast, looking to his right. He saw something in the house across the street. The window curtain moved. Behind Richard was the main road and the bar parking lot. To the left of him was the used car office. He had a strange feeling more story was to be found here. He walked back to the bar parking lot keeping an eye on the house where he saw the curtain move. He moved diagonally, walking like a white gowned model with a full glass of red wine. He pointed the camera in the direction of the house without lifting it to his face. He took a hip picture. He checked the zoom and adjusted it to bring an object closer. Richard stopped and pointed the camera right at the window and snapped another picture. The street corner sign read, Morgan Avenue. He fired off several more shots. He pushed the zoom button to gather distant objects as he crossed the street.

As he walked through the parking lot of Big Mike's Café, a girl was getting out of her yellow Ford Mustang. She had a white shawl around her shoulders. Her straight brown hair touched her shoulders. She had a black Texas cowboy hat in her hand. As she stood, Richard thought she was about one hundred ten pounds, maybe five foot, three inches tall. He could score her a perfect ten.

"How are you doing, Millie?" He spouted. Richard figured he would take a guess that this was Sandy's relief. He was right.

"Hello, mister. You're a new fella." she said.

"Sandy told me her relief was coming on duty about six o'clock. It's just about six now." As he spoke, a church bell sounded in the distance.

"Right on time," as she looked toward the church bell sound. She was as attractive as Sandy except not as tall.

"This is my lucky day," Richard told her.

"I've met two beautiful girls who know how to dress," He quipped. She smiled and continued to walk toward the bar entrance.

"Do you remember the bust at the used card lot a while ago?" Richard asks.

"Of course, that was a big deal around here. I bought a car from that low life," she said.

"Come on in and I'll tell you the details." She offers to hold the door for Richard. "Beauty before age," he said. With that, he holds the door and escorts her into the bar. Sandy waves as she can see they have met.

"Sandy, will you join me in a frosty?" He asks. "No, I've got an exam to take tomorrow, maybe another day." Richard wastes no time giving her more details as if to coach her into thinking again about his offer.

"I plan on leaving to chase the terrorists tomorrow. You might not get another chance to be with a bounty hunter," he says. Sandy stops for a moment. She turns and pours two mugs of beer and plops down next to Richard.

"Go ahead, mister bounty hunter, this one is on the house," she says. Richard talks about the bust in Ohio and tells them he plans to make a few busts himself.

"I was in on the whole operation. You could say I was a planted mole," he lied.

"I plan on collecting bounty money when I find these terrorists. I have an exceptional sensory nerve. I can detect the presence of people who mean to do us harm. The FBI says about ten of these guys are on the run. I'm going to find them.

"Millie, you met the owner of the used car lot. Sandy said you bought a car from him. Do you remember seeing anyone else hanging out around this business?" Richard asks. Millie says, "I told the FBI everything I could think of,"

"How often did you see cars being dropped off," asks Richard?

"The cars just show up," she says.

"Do you two know any of the neighbors around here?" Richard asks.

"We keep to ourselves," Sandy says.

Richard finishes another draft and asks Millie for another round. Sandy declines the offer and says she'll watch for him on the evening news when he captures the terrorists. He wishes her good luck on her test.

"I might be around for another day or so," says Richard.

"Millie, have you ever seen the neighbor across the street? I could swear I saw someone in the window of that green sided house on the corner." Richard says.

"That house has been empty for the last couple of months. I don't think anyone lives there right now." Millie replies.

"I'm going to stay parked in your parking lot tonight if you don't mind. I have to check out some things around here before I move on."

Richard is working on a sixth mug of beer. That was enough for him. He has a good place to work from so he decided to sleep in his van for the night. The thought of that curtain moving in the window, that made him a little curious.

He walks to his van as he watches the house across the street. He thinks he saw a flicker of light in the window.

As he sits in the van, he grabs his camera and zooms in on the window. The sun is down now. He keeps watching. He thumbs through the stored pictures in the camera. When he comes to the picture of the house across the street, he is aghast. The picture has a slight glow from the window where he saw the curtain move.

"Is this a reflection of light?" He asks himself. Twenty minutes passed by, the sun is gone. The street lights are lit. Richard moves the driver side seat into the recline position. The beer is working through his system. He exits the van and walks over to the bushes out of sight. It is a good spot to empty his bladder.

The street light is glowing now. He climbs back into his van and continues the surveillance. He saw another flicker of light as if someone is lighting a cigarette. He wonders if it was just a reflection of a car headlight. He keeps watching until he finally doses off and starts to dream.

The door of the house creaks as it closed. As Richard looks up, he sees a person leave the house. It is the house across the street. The man drops a cigarette on the ground and walks down the sidewalk away from him. He keeps walking away. His pace is fast. He is young, medium build and he isn't wearing a coat. His dark complexion makes Richard *think he is Negro except his hair isn't afro. He has a close cropped beard. The man didn't see Richard, as Richard is hidden from view, tucked away in the hedges.*

Richard's dream ends as a motorcycle barrels down the road. Four hours had passed and everyone is gone from the bar's parking lot.

The dream is still planted in his mind. He looks across the street. He can see the hedges behind the house where he dreamed he was hiding.

Richard decides to pick up where his dream ended. He would like to know more about his dream. He thought about the man. Was he a bad guy, a terrorist? Richard's dream sends a chill through him. He's going to wear his weapon. If only he knew what is going to happen.

"Damn that motorcycle, it fouled the dream."

Richard removes his jacket and changes to a dark coat to cover his holster. Being left handed, the right handed holster was awkward. He tries a fast draw of his pistol to see if this is going to be a hindrance. Richard is no Wyatt Earp. After a few attempts at extracting the gun he decides to stop before he shoots himself. He is smart enough to keep the gun unloaded. Now it is time to load the gun. He opens his suitcase and finds the pocket with the bullets. He picks out sixteen bullets and loads eight into the gun. He sticks the remaining eight bullets in his coat pocket.

The night air is cool. A light breeze is blowing from the west. Richard didn't want to slam the door on the van. He merely presses the door closed until he hears the door latch click. Walking across the street, the night is noticeably quiet. Not a soul is around. He makes his way to the back of the house being extra careful not to make any noise. The white tennis shoes don't agree with the stealthy approach he's making. Richard finds a place where he can hunker down. The hiding spot affords him, a good vision of the street and the back door of the mystery house. He didn't want his hiding spot to be a restroom but nature calls. As Richard unzips his fly, he hears a door open. He immediately reverses his course. This is not the time to urinate. A man exits the house. He is the man in the dream. Richard's dream is playing out.

He walks past Richard's hideout. He is fifteen yard from Richard as he advances across the yard. The man isn't wearing a coat which seemed unusual. His bearded face gives Richard the impression he must be about thirty years old. He moves fast as he looks both ways. The man swivels his neck. His shoulders stay parallel like a baseball pitcher watching a lead off runner. Richard can see the man is concerned about being seen. He has a cigarette cupped in his right hand. He gives a hard look around the back yard as he moves away from the house. Once on the sidewalk, he hustles.

Richard needs to come out from his hideout to keep an eye on the man. He grabs some loose dirt and tries smearing it on his tennis shoes. He doesn't want the tennis shoes becoming a beacon. Richard walks behind the man, giving him at least a fifty yard lead. He is careful to keep a few trees between him and his location. The man advances at a brisk pace. After two blocks, he turns left, down Lake Avenue. As Richard moves up to the corner, he watches the man enter a side door of a small store. It is a red brick delicatessen. He jots down the street address; one, one, twenty-one Lake Avenue. Mahdi Meat Market is on the store front. A black BMW sedan is parked near the store.

Richard watches the deli for a short while and then heads back to the first house. He steps into the bushes out of sight. Boldly, he walks up to the back door, opens the screen door and checks if he can turn the door knob. He can feel the door knob turn. The house is unlocked. At this juncture Richard doesn't know what to do. The house is dark inside. Richard decides he is setting himself up for trouble. He can't do it. He'll be trespassing. His excuse to himself is he needs to pee so he walks back to his van. After he unlocks the driver's side door, he walks around to the passenger side of the van and relieves himself. He walks back to the driver's side and hops into the driver's seat. He holds his hands over his ears. He wants to block out all distractions.

"Did I lose my nerve? What do I need to do? I'm going back to the house." He says quietly. He grabs a beer. Richard overcomes his fear by downing a beer. The liquid courage gives him a false boost.

"A bounty hunter has to take a few chances," he says.

With that, he must go back.

Once at the back door he looks to see if anyone is around. He feels safe. As he pushes the door, it creaks. The place is very dark. He always carries a small light and a pocket screwdriver. He has the light inside a sheath attached to his belt. The Velcro flap that covers the light makes a little tearing noise as he peels away the flap. He's holding his breath just hoping no one is home. He cups his hand over the light so as not to let a bright shine radiate inside the house. The back door leads to a stairwell and to the left are steps to the first floor. The stairwell goes down to the basement from this landing. A door is closed off to his left. He would have to go up five steps to get to that door. Richard looks behind as he shuts himself inside the house. He is careful not to make a sound. Scary, dark and creepy are words Richard thinks to describe his emotional state. He slowly creeps down the steps into the basement. The place has an odor of dampness and a zoo smell. There are two doors to his left that are closed. He sees feathers on the concrete floor in front of him. The basement room has a few cages on work tables. These are big cages, maybe three feet by three feet by four feet deep.

"What was that?" He whispers and freezes. Richard acts as if he has someone guarding his rear. He can hear a bird sound. It's the flap of wings he hears as a bird flies past him. He instinctively hits the deck fumbling for his hand gun. He's discombobulated. He tries to do a fast draw. Not succeeding with the draw he freezes to let things settle down. An occasional coo is heard as he gathers his wits. The basement is a sanctuary for pigeons.

The basement has a few boxes on the floor. It appears someone is either moving in or out. He sees benches with tools spread over them. A chemistry lab is set up on a table. It looks like someone is experimenting with gases and chemicals. There are small tubes hooked up to each other. They run from a small cylinder to a large upright cylinder. Richard checks the labels on the cylinders.

He hears a car outside. His heart is pounding as he listens. His predicament is giving him the shakes.

"What am I doing?" Richard asks himself.

One of the cylinders has a warning label on it. *This product is a health hazard, extremely dangerous if used in open air. A breathing apparatus is necessary when using this chemical. A nerve agent, SARIN, is produced when mixed.*

Richard sees white power inside a clear plastic bottle on the table.

That was enough for him. He is getting out of there. He starts up the steps, slowly climbing. As he gets near the top step, he sees a shadow of a person outside the door. He cups the light in his hand. Carefully, he backs down the steps as the person jiggles with the door handle. Without hesitating, the person gets inside and moves left going up the steps. Thankfully, Richard is not noticed as the person opens the first floor door. He can hear the door shut.

Richard is getting out. He works his way up the steps. He's inching along and finally reaches the back door landing. He opens the door ever so slowly. Time seems infinite as he fights to pry open the door.

"Please don't make a squeak."

Richard is calling out to God without saying a word. Finally, it opens, as he slips outside. He closes the door the same way without fully pulling it shut. That was good enough.

He walks away from the house in the direction of the Mahti Meat store. He is about fifty yards away from the house when he cuts across the street moving back toward the used car business. His pace quickens as he crosses the street to his van. Once at the door he unlocks the van and gets in. The mission was wild. He is totally flustered. Richard grabs a beer out of the cooler and twists off the cap. His hands are trembling as he downs the drink in three successive gulps. He's worn out, emotionally drained. The last hour on the job as a bounty hunter was hair-raising. Richard has one hell of a story already. This is an FBI matter.

He better shut down for the rest of the night. Daylight will be here shortly. He unloads his weapon and packs the equipment for another day. He fluffs the pillow on the floor of the van. When his head hits the pillow, the effect is like taking a sedative.

He falls asleep almost instantly. A dream races into his mind.

I see a man with a respirator covering his mouth and nose. He attaches a small plastic band on a pigeon's leg. He has many cages with birds inside. The man carries the bird up the steps. He opens the door and lets the bird take flight.

7

The Bird Bomb

Richard's short nap is enough to revive him. Before he forgets his dream, he grabs a piece of paper to write down a note. *They want to use birds. Birds are part of a plan to bomb people with chemicals*

Richard couldn't believe what happened last night. Already he had plenty of fresh leads into another sinister plot. Terrorists are using that house. Whoever is living there is planning another al Qaeda type mission.

"I'm going to think this terrorist plot through. This terrorist cell is planning on using birds, pigeons, to carry a mixture of chemicals. The question is this. How does he get the birds to cooperate? These people are nuts. What crazy religion are they practicing?"

Richard got on his knees to pray. He acted as if he was in church. He feared failure. Richard understands the problem. He has been at this crossroad before. If he goes into the bar again, he is liable to go overboard. The beer last night was good. For Richard, this is the hallmark of his problem. He has the disease. His weakness and lack of will power wins.

"God, help me overcome my fear." He asks God to help him.

Richard's method to detect the terrorists wins out. He needs to expose this terrorist menace. He is not a great religious person. He certainly is not a religious fanatic.

"Who on earth would poison people by aerial bird bombs," asks Richard.

He continued talking to himself. He knew Mahdi.

"I remember one of the terrorists, Mr. Abdul Mahdi. He was a well educated man. I believe some of his academia roots sprang from the Canadian education system. He had a spiritual air about him. He trained his pet parakeet to talk. He didn't really talk. The bird only made sounds like speech."

Richard thought about Mr. Mahdi. He met him at the convenience store in Fairport Harbor.

"He is in prison now. He could be helping his people but instead he became mixed up in exporting terrorism. All the time, effort, and money these terrorists are putting into harming humanity is unbelievable. Why can't the Muslim terrorists and guys like Mr. Mahdi, spend all of their energy building a better life for themselves? Can't they learn from history?" asks Richard. He talks out loud.

"The third world bullies can't see they are hanging above hell. If they look down, they will see charcoal cadavers of Hitler, Mussolini, and Ceausescu. The pit is full of other terror organizers such as Zarqawi and Saddam Hussein."

Richard snaps out of his historical menagerie. He better watch over the delicatessen for the next day or so. He will set up a stakeout near the building. He wants to see how many people come and go from that place. The terrorist may have made this town a staging ground. They did that in Ohio.

"This is operation BIRD BOMB," exclaims Richard.

He is going to wait a few days before he calls the FBI. He is going back to the bar today for another chat with the barmaids. Richard will ask them to keep an eye on the house across the street while he stakes out the delicatessen.

He hops into the driver's seat and starts up the van. He will patrol the neighborhood. Richard needs to familiarize himself with the layout of the town. He drives around in an ever widening circle, taking in the landmarks. Blasdell, New York wasn't too far from Buffalo or the Canadian border.

"Are the terrorists all over America?" he asks.

8

Bed and Breakfast

Richard stopped his van at a small park overlooking Lake Erie. The empty parking lot was a perfect place to contemplate his next move. It didn't take long to decide he needs a place to stay for the next few days. The fast developments of last night presumably discovering another terrorist cell meant he would need additional time to sort through the terrorist's game. Richard is in luck as he saw a bed and breakfast place for rent a few houses down and across the street from the Mahdi delicatessen. He will stakeout the delicatessen from there. He will go out on foot patrol during the day and do some investigating.

"FBI, we have another New York problem!" Richard, half rejoicing, cannot wait to tell the FBI.

Richard is going to sound the alarm bells as soon as he has sufficient info on the terrorist nests. In the one house he visited, someone is working on a dangerous experiment. Sarin gas is bad news. From what little Richard knows about sarin; it is a deadly substance. The delicatessen is probably a front for moving equipment and supplies to the house where the experiments take place. Richard wants to have enough information for the FBI so they can raid these places. Locate the nest, intercept, and destroy the operation, is Richard's code of conduct. There is one exception to this rule.

"I want to be long gone with reward money in my hand when the FBI arrives." Richard says confidently.

He crawls to the back of the van and lays out a beach towel. The van is not exactly a Holiday Inn but it is a place to rest.

Richard jokes. "The van is a rolling Holiday Inn. You can expect little or no sleep." It is still too early to check in at the bed and breakfast. He may as well try to sleep a couple more hours.

The van isn't that bad of a place to relax, but Richard could sure use a shower. If he runs into the girls at the café, they might get the impression he's a vagrant.

Richard opens his laptop computer and types down the sequence of events that took place over the past day. His recollection of the details is most important.

He looks away from the lap top to resume his stare at the roof of the van. He doses off for a little over an hour. Richard wake up to the sound of a street cleaning machine passing the park.

Outside was a view of Lake Erie to the West. There are sea gulls circling overhead. The lake birds must have gotten a whiff of the air in Richard's van. The smell in the van was annoying.

"I better take a shower," whispered Richard as if someone else was with him. His Sherlock Holmes type mission has him thinking of adding a partner. Richard would prefer a female companion but the way he operates makes the investigative job quite dangerous. He has his .22 Magnum pistol to keep him company but that's not exactly his guardian angel although it does afford him a little sense of security.

He put the holster back on and stuck the gun into it. A zipper coat is used to hide the weapon. He drives over to a local Mickey D's drive through and orders a coffee with a croissant breakfast sandwich. Pulling away to park, he wolfs down the breakfast sandwich. It is time to secure a temporary office. His hunt will start soon. The bed and breakfast inn is in a perfect spot.

A nice mannered woman greets Richard at the inn.

"I'm looking to stay three days. Do you have any rooms with a view to the West?" A slight smile is produced with his question.

She says, "Follow me. I have a thirty-five dollar per day special rate going on right now. Take a look at the room before we get into details."

She talks a little about the town.

"I've been here for thirty some years. Just call me Bee."

"I'm Richard Stern, a photographer and writer."

Lady Bee has a nice second floor room with a view of the deli across the street.

"This will be perfect!" Richard exclaims. He prepaid a hundred and five bucks. "This is a pretty fair price for three days," says Richard.

"Well mister, I don't have many customers here now," she explains as they start back to the front desk.

"Winter is coming, so you get a break," she says. "Don't bring any pets in here. Pets are not allowed. I had a problem a few years back and I made a rule, no pets. Another guest, Monica, is downstairs. She just registered. Monica is the quiet type. She's a receptionist at a library somewhere. You might get a date with her if you play your cards right."

This statement caught Richard off guard. He couldn't tell if she was just kidding. He put the comment into the back of his mind, thinking she might be helpful in the future.

"It's peaceful around here. Nothing happens in Blasdell, New York. It's a quiet town. A few merchant men come by every now and then. They must know someone across the street because they go to that deli to stay," says Bee.

"Really!" Richard exclaims. He got a little excited when he heard her mention the deli and men stopping to stay.

"Why, you have a clean operation here, Bee. Who could pass this place up," asked Richard. You must know everything that goes on around here." He was fishing for a comment. Bee has a watchful eye on her street. She reminded Richard of Mrs. Rutherford, the wise old lady on the Grand River back in Ohio.

Bee was ten years older then Richard. She's sixty, a stocky lady with legs made for a piano mover. She is single. Her husband is gone. The dress she was wearing made Richard think she was of European ancestry. It was a colorful pattern of flowers. It was a throw back to the fifties.

Richard signed the guest register and Bee hands him a couple of fresh towels.

"Thanks Bee, I'm in desperate need of a shower."

"Get yourself straightened up. You can join us for lunch at noon. If you can't make it, there's a twenty-four hour restaurant down the street," says Lady Bee.

"Please excuse my grubby look, Bee. I was working late last night and didn't get much sleep. The job takes me into some unusual places. I'm a freelance photographer and writer." Richard says apologetically.

She can see his sullied appearance.

"You have a shower in your room," she says.

It wasn't long after Richard took a shower and lay on the bed that he was asleep. It was almost noon, two hours went by. Richard decided to join Bee for lunch and quiz her about the merchants coming into Blasdell.

She had the table set for three. Richard assumed Monica would be joining them. His hunch was correct as Monica came into the room. She immediately introduced herself.

"Hello, my name's Monica Micovich. I'm an ad researcher and part time librarian. I'm working for a local news service right now. What about you, sir?"

"I am Richard Stern, the lion hearted, photographer and writer. I have been working on a new assignment for one day now. I research people and crime scenes."

Richard wouldn't reveal his exact mission.

He explained to Monica that terrorist activity was on the rise near the border with Canada. He was interested in bringing the public up to speed regarding border security. Their quick greetings broke the ice of stranger meeting stranger. Monica was a college educated girl. She was thirty-one. She was single and a knockout. Her face was radiant, clean and young looking. Richard felt attracted to her. He was old enough to be her dad. That was ok with him. He wouldn't want her doing dangerous work, especially bounty hunting. Richard didn't want a dame fouling up his bounty hunting.

Monica was interested in his work and she quizzed him as if she were taking a poll of his views. Her Edinboro, schooling was mixed with schooling in New York where she graduated from college, although she seemed to leave a void in her work experience after graduation. Richard guessed she took on menial jobs until she landed a career starter.

They dined on sour kraut and sausage. Bee said she was raised a Catholic. Richard thought she might be of Polish descent because of her menu.

"Bee, do you ever wonder about who comes into town?" he asked.

"I mean being by the border; are you concerned about terrorists?"

"No, this country has a way of settling almost every possible group in the land. Anyone that wants to make trouble in America usually gets caught." She said.

"We would have caught the 911 terrorists but the people teaching flying lessons were too greedy. I keep the eyes open. People who look suspicious and create trouble, they'll get caught and then the ACLU will save them." She says.

Richard thinks Bee injects the ACLU comment as if to say she is a right leaning Republican.

"Any terrorists around here, Bee?" Richard asks. He thought he could fire off this statement to see how Bee and Monica react.

"I watch the used car places now. That's where the FBI picked up a few terrorists. The place was called the Lemon Tree used car dealership. They were right here in town," says Bee.

"Bee, I do a little border patrol work in Ohio. My house is a few blocks away from Lake Erie. The terrorists set up shop in our grocery store. The FBI caught them. We had a major bust, so I'm on guard wherever I go. After going through that experience, I question little businesses that deal in food. The terrorists in Ohio were rooted in little ma and pa convenience stores. Who runs the deli across the street, Bee," asked Richard?

"That's Mustavi Mahdi," she says.

"Do you think he could be a terrorist?" asked Richard.

"Maybe, but we can't accuse everyone without proof. Just because he has a strange name doesn't make him a terrorist," she says. Bee didn't continue.

Richard suspected she didn't want trouble. Bee changes the subject. She had enough of terrorist talk.

"The weather has really been nice. Wouldn't you say September was a warm month, Monica?" Bee asks.

"It sure has been, Bee," says Monica.

Monica was taking in the conversation. She didn't inject anything until Richard brought up the deli across the street. Richard thought she might regard the terrorist subject as a topic like football. You are either a fan or don't give a hoot about what happens on a football field. Monica asked Richard if he would like to escort her over to the deli tomorrow. She said she would buy lunch for them from the deli across the street.

"Don't worry, Bee, Mr. Stern and I will check out the deli and make sure you don't have terrorists as neighbors."

"I have had enough of this nonsense from you two already," objected Bee.

She moved the subject to her past marital relations.

"My first husband was killed in Viet Nam just after we married. We were involved in high school and got married early. The Viet Nam war took Teddy. My second husband, Oscar, died from lung cancer. We were married for twenty years. Both husbands were smokers. The war got one and a bad habit got the other," she relates.

Bee served a nice dinner. They concluded their meal with coffee and a piece of cheese cake. Richard was happy with the opportunity to visit the deli.

"Monica, what time should we shop the deli tomorrow?" asked Richard.

"Knock on my door at eleven. When we are at the deli, I can decide on the menu. It might be submarines sandwiches for lunch tomorrow. Of course, that depends if we make it out alive." Monica had a sly smile on her face after that comment.

They finished their dessert and Richard thanked Bee for her hospitality. As he was leaving, he saw an opportunity to escort Monica to her room.

"See you tomorrow, Mr. Stern." With that, she closed the door.

Richard thought about what was said during lunch. Monica isn't a librarian. She seemed to enjoy the terrorist topic. He has a warm feeling. She would be a great friend.

9

Deli Stop

Richard figures he can have a few cocktails this evening. He might get a forecast about the deli visit tomorrow. He didn't want to drink too much so he stays in his room and rests. After feasting on Bee's lunch, he lies around and keeps tab on the deli. He has his camera at the ready in case he sees someone of interest. After seven o'clock, he takes another shower and is out the door by eight.

Richard drives to Mike's cafe and settles down on the end bar stool. This way he could talk with Millie the barmaid without customers listening in on his conversation. The bar business is a little slow. From his vantage point, he could see the house across the street. He decides swilling beers and making small talk with Millie is a comfortable way to bounty hunt.

Richard tries to fit in with the regular crowd as if he's a regular patron. His pool shooting is poor at best. One major problem, he is out of practice. Another real problem is his eye sight isn't what it once was. He challenges a young stud as if he is a hustler. Richard ends up buying the young man several beers before he finally gives up.

Richard needs to keep an eye on the house across the street so he returns to the end bar stool. Millie is looking mighty fine. The beers were helping accentuate her positives. The girls become more attractive as Richard drinks. This is one of the laws of the beer drinker. The girls are relatively attractive early on and damn beautiful by closing time. Richard is into his sixth beer desperately trying to slow down. He hasn't detect any action at the house.

The drunk in him was slowly rearing its head. He thought about Father Pete's words of wisdom. *'St. Jude can help but you must stop drinking.'* Richard needs to leave the bar before he reaches a state of no return. That point isn't too far off. He makes his get-a-way of sort without saying goodbye. He just feels compelled to leave after thinking about Father Pete's words and his problem with alcohol.

Father Pete's message helps deliver him back to Bee's place, however, not before he picks up a carry out twelve pack. Richard just has to stop at a convenience store. Once in the safety of his room, he pops open a beer and clicks on the tube. He didn't have a TV guide but the cable station gives him a preview of stations to view. An Indian western is just starting.

As he walks into the bathroom, he sees the Erie Indian image again. He hadn't seen him for the past few months while he was sober, and it was only a quick flash. The hallucination was a tell tale sign for Richard. He would soon be back to his old habit. Richard knows an alcoholic will resume old habits and return to where he was when he stopped drinking. One drink and he will have to drink until he is drunk. He fights the temptation to keep drinking.

He switches channels. He lies on the bed half asleep, trying to watch the 11 o'clock news. As he doses, he is greeted by a dream.

He saw a woman, an agent. She was meeting with several of her co-workers. They were planning a raid. She had her back to him. The clock on the wall indicated twelve.

"We need to know what is stored on the farm." She said.

Music sounded from the TV. The local station blasted an advertisement.

Richard wakes up as the show is playing a beer commercial. He grabs his pen and writes a note down. *Something will happen at a farm.* He does this so he will remember something of his dream. In ten hours, he would be meeting with Monica. He takes off his shoes and watches from the window to see if there is any action going on at the deli. He moves a chair over to the window and turns off the TV. He opens another beer in the darkened room. After a couple of gulps, Richard fades out. His head bobs a few times almost spilling the beer in his lap. His stakeout is over. He puts the beer down and climbs into bed.

Morning arrived. The TV was still playing. His mouth was dry. Richard could see the open beer can on the floor standing upright. That was a switch. Usually, he knocked it over before going to bed.

Richard did a couple stretching exercises before rolling out of bed. His head was still charged from the after effects of the beer. He looked at his watch. It was eight-thirty in the morning. He grabs some fresh clothes and takes a shower. He's OK after drinking a hefty amount of water. Considering the number of beers he had, he hopes he can stay sober for a day. He doesn't want to get the shakes from withdrawal. He opens up a Milky-Way candy bar for breakfast. He thought about asking Bee if she wanted to go out for breakfast.

"I better not though. I want to be ready to case out the deli with Monica." He says.

He walks outside to check on his van. While there, he picks up the lap top computer and camera. As he's pondering the situation, he decides to bring his .22

MAG to the room. Once in the room he sets everything on the bed. He checks to make sure the gun isn't loaded. He takes off his shirt and straps on the holster. A white tee shirt keeps the holster from chaffing his chest. As he is putting the shirt back on, he notices the bulge of the gun protruding from his chest.

"I can't go to the deli like this."

He puts on an overcoat. Thinking somebody will notice he's trying to hide something, he takes off the coat, shirt and holster. He slips the belt from the holster so that the pistol is only in the holster. Grabbing a sock, he wraps it through the belt loop on the holster. He lowers his pants to his ankles and ties the holster to the back of his leg above the knee.

"This is going to work," says Richard as he pulls up his relax fit jeans.

"I'm going to need time to lower my pants if I need to get my gun. I never said I was Elliot Ness," jokes the bounty hunter.

He will go through a rehearsal in case he needs to use the pistol. The mirror on the door reveals something seen in a comic book. His pants are dangling around his ankles. He has his weapon drawn.

"I'll be ready for the bad guys. Ha, ha, I'm the gun toting flasher," laughs Richard.

He loads the gun and put eight extra shells in his back pocket. He finally gets settled. It's about eleven o'clock. He walks over to Monica's door and knocks. She opens the door and greets him.

"Richard, you are right on time." She says.

"Are you ready, Monica?" asks Richard.

Her dark blazer matches her hair. She looks like a librarian. She's wearing dark rimmed eyeglasses.

"Let's go," she says.

"If these guys turn out to be terrorists, I'll let you handle it, Monica," says Richard jokingly.

"You steal the sandwich buns. I'll keep you covered," she says playing along with his joke.

They walk across the street and close in on the store front.

"Mustavi Meats, that sounds like an Italian name, like Mussolini," comments Richard.

The building is drab, in need of a paint job. Inside the display window are several stuffed birds perched on tree limbs. Old butcher block tools adorn the display. A sign says, 'We undress your hunting game. Deer, boar, and turkey, are no problem.'

Richard sees a parrot is alive inside a huge cage. The smell of pepperoni flavor is in the air. The front door creeks as he opens it. Many food prices are posted at random. He notices the old wood floor hasn't seen wax in years. The store is loaded with shelves of dry goods. A flag is tacked on the wall. The caption below the flag reads, 'I'm from a foreign land just like Columbus.'

"They might be Italian, Monica."

Monica heads over to the counter of cold cuts. As she walks away from Richard, he remembers the woman's figure from the dream.

"Is Monica, the woman agent in my dream?" He thinks to himself.

Richard starts to case the place out. One man is following him and two men work with Monica. Monica orders two different half pounds of ham. One is honey baked and the other is smoked. Richard asks the attendant if he has fresh submarine buns. He takes Richard toward Monica. In front of the deli counter is the bread. Richard picks out a package of eight buns. They pay for the goods and head back to Bee's place.

"They might be terrorists," says Richard.

Monica laughs and says, "You're dreaming."

10

Second Search

Richard had lunch with the women for the second time. Monica and Richard chatted about the non-event. Their adventure together, shopping at Mustavi Meats, was as exciting as washing dishes. Monica was artful though. She picked up on banners and posters of Middle Eastern scenes. The flags on the walls were Iranian, Iraqi, and Syrian.

Monica is well read. She talked about attorney and detective shows and books. Sherlock Holmes cases intrigued her. Richard became all the more interested in her real job which she talked about sparingly. Richard had a suspicion she was part of a greater organization like the FBI. Her body was in great physical shape.

As evening came, Richard decided he would pay another late night visit to the house by the used car lot. He watched TV for a while and drank a few beers. He wrote a letter about the deli using his lap top computer. As he wrote, he focused on the tie between the mystery house and the man who walked to the deli from the house.

He set the alarm clock on his watch for one o'clock in the morning. He had some time on his side so he downloaded the camera pictures onto the lap top. The lap top had a number of old photos stored on it so he reviewed those. He brought up the new pictures of the mystery house. As he clicked through each frame, he came to the shots where he varied the zoom. As he inspected the photos, he highlighted the top of the house. He saw a number of birds hovering near the chimney. The birds were big, nothing like a sparrow or even a black bird.

"They're pigeons," exclaimed Richard.

He closed down the software running the pictures. The Olympus took decent pictures considering he was on the move when he took those pictures.

His watch beeped to signal him. It was show time. He purposely wore dark clothes as he left Bees. The espionage work was an overlooked part of bounty hunting. He didn't realize he would need to do so much late night prowling.

Richard walked around the block working up his nerve. He would need to trespass again. He had the beer courage in his system.

"You know, Stern, you're out of the box, gather your senses if you have any. This is a job for the FBI. This investigative work is plenty scary. You better call upon a greater power. Why don't you have a few more beers?" He whispered.

Richard knew he was throwing out security. Now he used an old motto.

"One step for man and one giant step for a blockhead," said the bounty hunter.

"I have confidence, luck, and a big yellow streak running down my back. St. Jude, please hangout with the alcoholic. They won't take you to jail. So, if you have some spare time, just hangout with me tonight," prayed the bounty hunter.

Richard moved closer to the target house preferring to hide in the bushes again. The place was dark. He didn't think anyone was home. He stayed hidden for what seemed like hours. In truth, it was only an hour when the same man emerged from the house and walked in the direction of the deli. He kept an eye on him until he was well down the street. Then he decided the time had come to prowl. He walked up to the back door and tried opening it. It was locked this time. He had a small pocket screwdriver that he used on his camera and worked the lock plunger on the lock. It released.

"Holy Cow, St. Jude. Don't run away now."

Once inside the house, he maneuvered down the steps. He used his mini light to help guide him down the basement steps. He reached the bottom step and looked into the room that had the chemistry equipment. The stuff was gone. The equipment had been cleared from the room. Everything was gone. No cages, no boxes, everything was gone.

He walked up the steps and opened the other door to the first floor. Some light was shining in from the street lights. He moved forward imitating a church mouse. The house looked cleaned out.

He smelled an odor not like the basement bird coop. The odor was more than that. It was a gas. He remembered how propane smelled.

"It was propane!" gasped Richard. As he moved closer to the next room, he tried holding his breath. The smell became overwhelming. He shined his light on the living room floor. There was a propane heater hissing with a plastic milk jug sitting right next to it. Whatever was in the milk jug it wasn't milk.

"Jesus, this place is going to blow."

Richard reversed his position as he heard the whoosh sound of ignition. The heat of the air igniting was at his backside. His mad dash to the backdoor was accomplished as if St. Jude had picked him up and threw him to the door. A flash lit the room, which cast his silhouette on the wall as he made it to the door going outside. He was moving at breakneck speed. In a huffed, rolling roar the house became a giant ashtray. Smoke and flame seemed to fly through the air. Window glass was bursting and landing in the bushes. The wood frame house became engulfed in flames. The scene was akin to a napalm bomb exploding. The heat of the flames was so intense Richard thought he was the stuffed pig spinning at a barbecue roast. The sound of the wood framed house losing its integrity made a snapping sound. Wood studs strained to contain the weight of the second floor. Richard double-timed his pace from the house fire. His legs turned into those of an Olympic sprinter. He made it to Bee's house out of breath as sirens burst to life.

The first beer went down in short order. He cracks the tab on another beer and grabs his camera. After a few sips, he set the can down and runs out the door with camera in hand. He decides to drive over to the house and see what's left. The police are diverting traffic away from the area. Richard pulls over and walks closer to the fire scene. He watches from a distance, memorizing the layout of the land. He snaps a few pictures in a panoramic sweep.

The fire department pours water on the blazing house. The embers remind him of a charcoal grill hours after the end of a party.

"Somebody deliberately torched this house," said the shaken bounty hunter. He can't become an accessory of the facts in this case. If he says he was here, he would become the person of interest.

"What do I do now?" asks Richard. He is in the middle of a crime scene. He knows the facts. As he watches the action, a black BMW sedan slowly passes by. The driver is the bearded man who left the house. He looks directly at Richard. Their eyes engage, almost taking a simultaneous picture of each other. Richard turns to avoid a stare. He hip shoots a camera shot of the car moving down the road. The driver pops his head out the window looking back at him. A feeling of danger runs goose bumps on his arms. Richard can feel the presence of evil.

He scrambles back to his car and then to Bee's place.

He writes a note on a pad. Then he types the note onto his lap top computer. "The FBI will need to know the facts. They can have this story but I'm looking to get some money for being an informer."

Richard will explain how the house fire is related to the delicatessen.

Dear FBI Agent Roman,

Please read this letter about a series of events that took place in Blasdell, New York. The Morgan Avenue fire in late September was set by a bearded man driving a black BMW sedan. He is somehow tied to a scheme to drop chemicals using birds, (pigeons). A delicatessen at one, one, twenty-one Lake Avenue is tied to terrorists. This lap top contains pictures that support this letter. Remember who gave you this tip. Reward money will help cure a bad memory. I'll find out more.

Bounty Hunter,
Richard D Stern

Richard tears the note from the note book, folds it up, and sticks it in his wallet. He is in the middle of a terrorist plot again. He will move on from here.

He lies down on the bed to rest for a few minutes. It didn't take long for another dream to appear.

Richard sees a sign that reads Syracuse, New York. A skeleton is hitchhiking. The boney corpse is flashing a cardboard sign. The sign says Washington, DC.

Richard Stern sees a sign over a bridge. It says, right turn Lincoln Memorial. The ground near the memorial is covered with pigeons.

11

BMW Follows Van

Richard says goodbye in a hurry. His quick departure surprises Monica and Bee. He says Interstate 90 East is the direction he is heading.

"Washington, DC is the next stop. Information received in the last couple days makes it imperative I leave right away."

"You should hang out a couple more days, Richard. We enjoy your company. We can shop some other stores. Maybe you'll find some terrorists. Look at all the potential terrorist problems you will miss." Monica presses him, pleading her case.

"The news said we have an arsonist in our neighborhood. Doesn't that bother you? Don't you want to know what happens?" asks Monica.

Richard fishes a note out of his wallet as he talks about his next move. He is anxious. So excited, he hands Monica five bucks as a tip.

"Oops, an emergency job came up. This necessitates the reason to leave right away. Everything is packed and the van is fueled. It is time to journey to the next story. You and Bee may read about it someday. Thanks for of your help and hospitality. By the way Monica, this note is for the FBI. It needs an envelope and stamp. Please mail it to the Cleveland FBI."

Monica unfolds the note and glances down to read it.

Richard starts his van. Driving down the street, he gives a final blast on the horn. Monica turns to Bee.

"What a nice guy, Bee! You hold down the fort. Something needs to be done right away. Talk to you later."

Bee was caught off guard by all the evacuations.

"You two should slow down. Listen to Bee, young lady. The world is too hectic. Richard talks about terrorists and you seem to enjoy that nonsense. Why don't you try sewing a quilt or painting a picture? That is relaxing," says the innkeeper. Bee watches, as they depart. Monica moves at a fast pace. She places a call to Agent Roman but the answering machine picks up her call.

"Mr. Stern is heading to Washington, DC. I have to go."

Richard is a hundred miles down Route 90, heading east. He has an uneasy feeling about terrorists plotting greater misfortune in America. As he travels down the interstate highway, he periodically looks in the rear view mirror to see advancing traffic. Of interest is a black car that has been hanging behind him. He noticed the car thirty minutes ago.

Richard is a little on edge because of the look he received from the man in the black BMW. The car following him looks suspicious. Almost like the car that the terrorist was driving in Blasdell.

He drives a little faster than the speed limit. His pace continues another fifty miles with no change. The car behind continues to follow. Richard plans a diversion. He could just turn around at a service truck crossover. He sees a truck stop is ahead. Here is where he can determine if the car is friend or foe. Richard pulls off the interstate and into the truck stop. He parks in front of the restaurant but in an end parking spot. This is right of the restaurant but still in view of the front door to the eatery.

He grabs his holster and shells as if he expects trouble. He stuffs the holster inside of his coat and walks to the restaurant. A panhandler is outside the front door asking for spare change. The hitchhiker is scamming for money. Richard flips him a quarter. Once inside, Richard walks to the men's room. A stall is open and he sits on the toilet seat. He takes off his coat and places the gun and holster on a hook.

Richard needs a strategy. He fidgets with the shells as he starts to load his pistol. Finishing this task, he dons the holster and gun. Next, he puts on his coat. His hands are trembling. He grabs his shaking legs. Richard could use a drink. His courage is on the lam. He steps out of the stall and leaves the men's room.

Richard watches outside for the BMW. Watching through the front door window, Richard sees the hitchhiker. He is still outside hustling incoming customers. This adds to a plan he quickly contemplates. Richard pounds on the entrance door window to get the hitchhiker's attention. The hitchhiker points to himself. Richard waves for him to come inside. The man opens the door.

"Hey pal, can you help me?" Richard asks.

"A twenty dollar bill is for you if you drive that blue Ford Aerostar van at the end of the row to the opposite side of this restaurant." Richard points.

"It is parked right there on the end parking space. I have a little girlfriend problem. I want my girlfriend to think I'm leaving. She's over there at the fuel pumps getting gas. If she sees that I'm leaving, she will think I'm headed back to the interstate. Just honk the horn and wave as you pass the gas pumps. The other girlfriend is working here and I don't want a cat fight. If the two ladies meet in here, I'll have a mess on my hands. Here, put on this hat. She will think you are me," says Richard.

Richard hands the man his hat, keys and flashes the twenty at him.

The man reached for the twenty.

"Not so fast, after you move the van, you get the twenty," says Richard. Just move the van to the other side of this building. That is all you have to do. Move it where she can't see the van. You get the twenty when you bring the keys back. It is that easy."

The hitchhiker saw easy money coming. He walks out the door and struts to the van. Richard watches as a black BMW car passes in front of the restaurant.

"Holy Mackerel! Please help me, St. Jude." Richard pleads to the guardian angel.

Two men in the car look very much like bad guys. As the hitchhiker hops into the driver's seat, an explosion erupts. The van does a giant leap into the air. Fire consumes the interior. The van is awash in fire. The hitchhiker is toast. He is killed instantly by the blast. The rush of patron in a chaotic charge pushes Richard outside.

He looks to see if he can help. The scene is similar to car bomb explosions in Baghdad. Richard's van is destroyed. Richard is quickly brought back to reality.

The BMW backs toward the car fire. A man jumps from the car and points a gun at Richard. Frightened, Richard makes a lame attempt to unfasten his coat. No such luck, he is clumsy as a year old baby. The man has a bead on Richard and a shot is fired. Richard holds his eyes closed. Another shot rings out. Richard looks at himself. He is surprised to see a man lying on the ground. A gun is several feet from him. The BMW squeals. The tires are spinning wildly.

"Richard, get in the car! Richard, hurry, get in this car!"

Richard is in shock.

"Monica!"

Monica is in rescue mode. She is driving her own car. She just shot a man. Her pistol is on the front seat as Richard climbs into the front seat.

"Holy cow! Monica! Holy cow, Monica," said the totally frightened bounty hunter. Richard was beside himself. The shock of the moment is withdrawing like a wave on Lake Erie's shore. He says a silent prayer as Monica accelerates her car. Monica heads east on the interstate. Monica is in complete control.

"Holy cow, Monica, you shot that man!"

12

Road Rage

"Monica, God sent you. You shot that man. Who are you? What the heck is going down? You are not just an ordinary citizen! You're no librarian, a pollster, no way. You carry a gun. Jesus, Monica! Jesus Monica," he exclaimed!

Richard was all over the place. He couldn't get his thought process together.

He was searching for answers. His mind was racing. Out of the clear blue sky this woman appears and guns down a terrorist. His answer, as he does so often, is easy.

"I need a beer," he claims.

"Monica, drive to a store, a bar."

"You need a shower, Richard. That will help you relax. You're involved with dangerous people. We are watching after you. The less you know about the way we operate, the better for you."

Monica pulled out her FBI identification and flashed it at Richard.

"I'm going to drive to a safer location and get you out of harms way. Another agent is tracking the black BMW. The message you sent to Agent Roman was enough to convince him that you need protection. He alerted us. Agents Roman and Wright felt you are in over your head. As a result, we will pop up if the situation warrants. We penciled you into our master plan to thwart terrorism. The FBI believes in your ESP."

"Well right now is a good time to start testing me. Let's work on my emotional stress right now. You can take me out for a drink. That is a good start," Richard replies.

He was adamant about needing alcohol. His disease was progressing again. While Richard's alcoholism was flaring, he refused to admit it. This cycle of habit is all too familiar. Once he starts drinking, it is always the same. He knows all alcoholics face this dilemma.

Monica was cognizant of the vehicles around her. She was cool and content motoring down the road, watching the rear view mirror. She looks at her watch every now and then. Richard thought, "It wasn't that long ago I was protecting her."

Richard thought about the man he sent to his van back at the plaza. He was the unfortunate one. What a bummer of a day for him. The people Richard is chasing are turning the table on him. He's the hunted one. All of his equipment is lost. His poor van is gone. Bounty hunting cost him a van.

"I'm in a real fix now. I don't have a van, a camera, or a laptop. Can it get any worse?" questions Richard. He sounds like a moaning Democrat after the Bush/ Gore presidential election.

"It can get worse. I think someone is following us," Monica adds.

"A car about a quarter mile back, just might be the bad guys. They are keeping their distance. Richard, we can see some people do not like you. Do you have trouble making friends? Do you hang with the wrong crowd?" questions Monica.

"Monica, I'm a regular guy. I know you are trying to calm the situation. Do you think the terrorists know I'm homing in on their game?" Richard guardedly asks.

He looks at her in a dazed way. He's waiting for her to be honest with him.

"Just tell me to bend over and kiss my ass goodbye," says Richard.

She might be used to being on the receiving side of gunfire but Richard is not. Richard's adrenal gland was pumping again. He is searching for an answer to his double conundrum. Richard is the hunted bounty hunter. He lost his tools. Poor Richard is without a van, clothes, camera, or a laptop computer to record his journey. He has one thing going for him. The FBI is giving him protection.

Monica responds to his frightened look as she can see the worry on his face. She breaks him from the dire thoughts with attention commands.

"Mr. Stern, you listen to me."

"I like you Richard. Your business plan stinks. We have to work together. We are partners right now. Bounty hunting is not your line of work. We are on the defense. I suggest you might try some other type of work down the road. Let me see. I know. You should be a soldier, an Army man," she says.

"What would I do in the Army?" I ask.

"Yes, the Salvation Army," she says with a laugh. "You need an occupation that is friendly, charitable. What I'm seeing is a man without a friend. Do you have close friends?" she asks.

"Father Pete is my friend. Can you find a better friend than a Catholic priest? I sure wish he were here. At least he would offer a prayer for the moment."

"I'm going to pull off at the next exit, Weedsport and Fort Bryon. I'll be able to tell if that car is friend or foe," Monica decides.

"Good, I'm going to buy a six pack. That's my friend right now. My bounty hunting days are over. This job can get a man killed."

Richard is a bit remorseful. He couldn't throw in the towel without a fight. His high expectations that he had for bounty hunting, seemed to vanish.

Monica took the exit and drove to a large multi-purpose gas station. She was keeping guard as Richard walked into the store. He went straight to the beer section. He grabbed a six-pack of sixteen-ounce cans and paid for the goods. He looked out the store window. If the black BMW car was anywhere in sight, he was staying inside the store.

Monica was fueling her car and next to her was another car of the same make as the one she was driving. Monica was talking to a sharp looking babe standing next to her. This girl had black hair, a tanned face, and was about the same size as Monica. Since they were talking out in the open, Richard decided the coast must be clear. He walks out and acts like a person who is in control of his destiny.

Monica called out.

"Mr. Stern, I want you to meet another friend of ours. I would like you to meet Paula Gavalia. She will be driving ahead of us. She is part of your protective package."

"Girls, would you mind telling me where we are headed?" Richard asks.

"Mr. Stern, you are getting special protection. You follow our instructions. You have opened a hornet's nest. The people you are after will harm you. Our duties for the FBI include surveillance and personal protection. I don't want to tell you too much. The protection wing of the FBI is working to keep you safe. That is what you need to know right now. Where we go is a secret," says Monica.

The beautiful Paula reinforces Monica's words, "I took care of the BMW following behind you. Their tires went flat and they are losing coolant. That is going to slow them down." She says with a smile.

The two girls had an air of confidence about them. The FBI sent a team of agents to protect Richard. The scene back at the plaza was a good indicator as to how dangerous his work has become. In Richard's opinion, the FBI certainly sent the right people. Being around girls with guns is cool, especially these two girls. They could easily pass for models in any beauty pageant.

"We're going to get you to a motel for today. Paula has a room already reserved for tonight. Tomorrow we move again. We want you to disappear, Mr. Stern."

"Well that sounds pretty good. Let's keep me above ground if you know what I mean. I would like to reappear down the road."

13

Hotel Shower

Monica and Paula set up a two-stage plan. They wanted to get Richard out of the limelight for a couple days as they put together a more permanent plan. They chose a mid-size motel/hotel called the Eighty-Inn. This eighty-room motel offered observation from four floors. The complex was only two miles away from the interstate highway.

Monica and Richard stopped at a McDonalds for a sandwich. He downed two sixteen ounce cans of beer while sitting in the car.

"OK, Paula, I'll make a switch at 5:00PM," Monica said as she ended her conversation. She put her cell phone into the leather holder clipped to her belt.

"Richard, I'm going into the ladies room. When I come back, we are going to drive next to that panel van over there. You are going to step out of this car and get into that van. The van driver is going to drive to the hotel where you will go to the second floor room 201. The room will be open."

"That sounds good to me Monica."

Richard was content. Really, he was at their mercy. His emotional high subsided after the beer got into his system. He popped open another beer as Monica walked to the restroom. She was looking nice. What a well-sculptured babe, he thought. His conscience complained that he was twenty-five years older then she. After about three minutes she came out. It was time to make a switch. She started the car and turned to him.

"This is a precautionary move, Richard. We are going to get you to a safe location where you can take a shower."

She winked at him and drove to the far side of the van. The large sized van obscured her car. Richard stuck his open beer can in his inside coat pocket. In the other two outside coat pockets, he stashed the other cans. Richard went from the car to the van in a swift exchange. The driver looked familiar as she backed out keeping her face hidden from him. He saw her face as she adjusted the driver's side mirror.

"Paula, is that you?" Richard asked.

She was wearing white coveralls. Paula had changed into a painters outfit, complete with hat. Her baggy uniform did a good job of concealing her figure. The passenger exchange was accomplished flawlessly.

"Were you expecting Leonardo DaVinci," asked Paula?

"You FBI folks are all set for Halloween," Richard said. She nodded in agreement.

"It is October you know. I like this month. We can use different disguises and pretend we're going to a Halloween party. You will see we have more tricks."

She pulled away as Richard watched the car he was riding in pull away. A dummy passenger was in the front seat of the car.

"We put Charlie in the seat where you were. We call him *Nine Lives Charlie.* He's there one minute and gone the next. We can blow him up and deflate him in seconds."

They got to the hotel in five minutes.

"Go to Room 201 now," said Paula.

Off Richard went, up the steps. Room 201 was right there. He walked right in. It wasn't a problem so far. The first thing he thought about is a shower. Oh, how he could use a shower and a nap!

"Nice accommodation," he said, listening for an answer. Richard wanted to make sure nobody else was lurking.

He looked around the spacious room. It had a small kitchen off to the side. The window in the kitchen faced a back parking lot. He looked outside in both directions to see if anyone was watching. A dozen cars were parked out back. He eventually turned his attention to the bathroom. That was his main objective.

Richard hung his coat up after he put the cans of beer in the refrigerator. The motel room was very nice.

"This is a seventy-five dollar room. I say this is maybe a three or four-star hotel. The FBI isn't going to stick me with a motel bill. Now if Paula and I are sharing this room and that bed, I will pay the bill. I will definitely pay the bill," he whispered naughtily.

Richard decided to do a quick brainstorm of events before he takes a shower. He grabs a motel room note pad and pen and commences to jot down a to-do list.

"What needs to happen?" he asks himself.

"The first thing I need to do is get the girls' cell phone numbers. If I have FBI protection, I want to call them if I get into a jam."

He starts to draw a map of the places he just traveled.

"Before I go any farther it is time for a beverage."

Richard grabs the open can and another beer that he put in the fridge. He downs the open one and pops the tab on the next beer. He starts to chart the terrorist movements. From Fairport Harbor to Buffalo, he draws what he suspected was their operating zone. His map of Lake Erie isn't exact but it is a close rendition. As he draws, he makes notes to detail what is taking place.

Richard finishes a fourth beer, only two left. He is getting a little tipsy so he lies on the bed. His eyes close and his rest turns into a deep sleep. The day's event and the beers culminate to trigger a strong dream.

The Erie Indian has an eagle perched on his muscular arm. His quiver and bow is slung behind him. He sends the eagle aloft. The eagle flies above a farm.

A tapping noise broke the dream. Richard tosses for a moment and fells asleep again. He wakes to a noise again but is too sleepy. His eyes close.

A man is walking to Motel Eighty. He knocks on the door. After knocking a second time, he leaves a package at the door. The man turns and reveals the room number on the door. It is room 201. Agent Paula walks up the steps and sees the man. She yells at him.

"Hey, what's in the package?" asks Paula.

Instantly, he turns, half startled. After one look at Paula, the man starts running away. He races down the other side of the building. Paula backs down the steps and watches the man run from the building. She starts after him, jogging at a medium pace. A black BMW is idling nearby. The man runs to the car.

"FBI, stop where you are," she commands!

The BMW pulls ahead as the man jumps into the passenger seat. The car hooks left through the parking lot and onto the roadway. Paula watches from a distance as she gives up the chase. She turns around and grabs her cell phone. She calls the front desk.

"Motel Eighty, front desk, Mr. Jenkins here, may I help you."

"Room 201, please hurry," she pleads!

"One moment," he says.

"Hurry," she commands!

Richard's room phone is ringing as he wakes from a rather vivid dream. He rolls to the phone half asleep. On the line is Paula talking in a frantic voice. Her voice sounds winded as if she ran a race.

"Richard, stay in your room. Don't go near the front door. Go to the bathroom and lock the door," she demands.

"What's going on," Richard asks?

"Never mind right now, do what I say. Do it now! Hang up and go to the bathroom, do it now!" Paula accelerates her pace, running full speed toward

Richard's room. She is at the other side of the building when a boom sends a cloud of smoke off the balcony ten doors away. The shock causes Paula to dive from the steps to the ground.

Richard walks over to the bathroom and closes the door behind him. Just as the door shuts, a boom goes off. The motel shakes sending Richard against the bathroom wall. He falls, half dazed. He's on the bathroom floor. His ears are ringing and he hears the alarm system wailing. The sprinkler system activates. Almost immediately, smoke seeps into the bathroom at the bottom of the door. Water is spraying in the bathroom from a ruptured sprinkler head.

Richard has to wrestle with the bathroom door in order to get it open. Water is spraying throughout the room. The room is in a shamble. The front door is blown off. Minor fires are spread about the room. Richard runs over to the kitchen window away from the main quarters. He struggles to open the window. The smoke is choking. He grabs a chair and smashes the window glass. Fear and panic creep inside his body. His adrenalin gives him a boost. His body strains, his strength drains by the overwhelming smoke. He grabs the tablecloth and lays it over the window edge. Reactively, he pushes the table to the window and slides his body to the window. The cool air is rushing inside. Slowly, he works his feet through the opening to lower himself. His drop to safety is cushioned by the fresh tilled ground.

Sirens are coming closer. People mingle in the back parking lot as others come running around the building. Richard lay on the grass for about ten seconds trying to figure out what's next. Someone yells to him.

"Richard, Richard, let's go," she says. Paula is ready with the car. She drove the car onto the grass. She jumps out of the car and run over to Richard.

"Can you move," asks Paula?

"I'm OK."

"It's time to go. We don't have any friends here," says the agent.

"We'll mail them a check. Now is not the time to lodge a protest over the accommodations. This motel is not smoke free." She candidly says.

"The room is overrated but the fireworks seem real," adds the slightly intoxicated Richard.

His humor is well placed as Paula positions herself to help.

Paula grabs his arm and helps him to his feet. They walk briskly to the car. She runs around to the driver's side after stuffing him into the passenger seat. Paula drives out of the parking lot almost in slow motion. She doesn't create a stir as folks begin to congregate.

"Richard, you need a shower."
They look at each other, half smiling.

14

Washington, DC

Richard thought something unusual about Monica. She could be part of a federal organization tracking down the terrorist escapees. He was right.

The FBI was searching for remaining terrorists that escaped from the Ohio and New York busts. The Mahdi Meat Market was just one piece of the puzzle that the FBI had their sights on. Agents Monica Micovich and Paula Gavalia were just starting an undercover stakeout in Buffalo. It was a coincidence that Richard Stern picked Bee's Bed and Breakfast as his place to stay. Agent Micovich was already there. Richard Stern merely added more work for the FBI. He complicated their investigation, although he was aiding the FBI with his information.

Supervisor Moses expressed surprise when he heard Stern arrived on the scene. Moses was aware of the tips Richard Stern supplied, but not about him being in Buffalo.

"He is what?" Moses asks

"He wants to be a bounty hunter. He believes the FBI will pay him reward money," says Agent Roman.

"Stern is trouble. He is not a bounty hunter. He is an FBI informer. That is all. Al Qaeda will shoot him dead," said Supervisor Cliff Moses.

"Paula and Monica can work together protecting this moron while you and Agent Wright investigate the Parkersburg, used car business. We need Stern's information. Stern is to cease all bounty hunting," says Supervisor Moses.

"The terrorist trail is moving to Washington, DC according to the information Monica has supplied. We have it covered, boss. Monica is guarding Stern and Paula is trailing them in another car.

Agent Roman adds, "I knew you wouldn't go for Stern's bounty hunting. I already spoke to Monica. She will relay the message to Stern about bounty hunting."

US 90 to US 81 South

Monica takes over driving again.

"I want you to know I'm mighty grateful for what you did back there. You saved my life. Thank you for risking your life. St. Jude should be St. Monica," says a grateful Mr. Stern. Monica looks at Richard as if to say, 'you're out of your league with these despots.'

"Richard, the ring leader is on the loose. We still need your uncanny ability. If you find this al Qaeda member, let the FBI do the arresting. We want to take him out before they have a chance to reconstitute. We think they are developing a third cell in America. We believe a man called Captain Awad is running the second cell. He escaped with his partner, Mr. Barrie."

"Monica, how long have you been following me?" asked Richard.

"We put a watch on you since you left the hospital in Willoughby, Ohio. The doctor there is psycho-analyzing your behavior. He's convinced you haven't been cured of your hallucinations."

"We don't follow you everywhere. If you are working a dangerous role, such as a bounty hunter, you will stop immediately. Our boss now knows this. What he means is this. As you get close to these people, they are going to try and kill you. Do you get the picture? The terrorists are on to your meddling. Our group understands the role you are following. We are not encouraging you to continue. Until you recover from alcoholism, you may continue to expose the terrorists. Since you're not ready to drop the alcoholic cross we are compelled to use your information."

"You helped us find the terrorist boats, a few cell stores, and you were quite specific as to the time and place of the terrorist mission in Fairport Harbor. As crazy as this is going to sound, going through life as an alcoholic is habitual punishment, but it is a service to the country."

Richard listened to Monica. She had explained a difficult topic. She remembers the high number of problems her peers faced when they abused alcohol in high school and college. Her message was to enjoy recreation, not recreational drugs.

"The FBI needs your input. A personal thought is that you can get better. Your life will have more meaning if you refrain from alcohol."

"Hold on, Monica! Doing bounty hunter work is an effort to make money. The meaning is green with presidents' faces on the paper. The messages come from the effects of the booze. The dreams lead to criminals. I'm out to collect a few rewards for my hard work in the bar." Richard winked to reassure Monica.

He realizes the wasted life an alcoholic travels. Richard makes an effort to condone the slovenly attitude. The truth is his family had a long line of heavy drinkers that stretched back to both grandpas. He was following the patient disease. The alcohol was a convenient way of helping the FBI but it masked a growing problem for Richard.

"I hate to over indulge but heavy drinking can lead to rewards," says Richard sarcastically.

"You will get the rewards, Richard, but bounty hunting is over. What we are trying to do is make sure you don't get wasted by the bad guys. Richard, your body will revolt one day. Take a new stand in life. Money should never be a reason to risk your health. I think deep down, you're a nice guy."

Richard was spellbound by her southern accent. Her voice came across loud and clear. With her words, Richard was beaming ear to ear. He wanted to show that he could overcome his problem. Inside, there was agony. He would admit the truth to her.

"You seem sincere, Monica. Hey, when helping this country, I'll just have to wet my whistle from time to time. The trouble is once I start, I can't stop."

"We know that Richard. We would like to end the terrorist mission in short order. Help us catch these losers and you can work on recovery. You are receiving protection twenty-four seven as of now. Call me a security blanket."

"Now you are talking. This is a good idea. Just how close will the security blanket cover me?" asked Richard.

Monica was professional. She pointed with her finger and with the other index finger gave a shame on you sign. Her Dallas, Texas hat covered her black shoulder length hair. She could easily pass for a magazine cover model.

The crime fighter and bounty hunter traveled for hundreds of miles. Richard dosed. His on and off sleep would keep him from understanding where they were. He woke up as Monica talked on her phone.

Monica had a computer screen mounted in her car. The new device, that Agent Wright installed, is working well. She follows a blinking dot on the screen. The blinking dot is traveling a full ten miles ahead. This goes on for miles.

"This target is another al Qaeda suspect. The terrorists were at the truck stop where we had the trouble. An RFID was attached to their car as they drove from the parking lot at the rest stop. We are now following them." She explained

They followed the al Qaeda connection to Washington, DC. The intercepted terrorists didn't know the female agent had bugged their car. Monica closed the gap between the two cars and got a visual on them inside the city limits. The suspect car's passenger was pointing to the driver to turn down side streets. He was purposely having the driver change lanes as if he knew the FBI was following.

Monica had excellent driving skills. She pulled over and gave them plenty of lead time. They still had the tracking device monitoring the terrorist's car. They could resume contact with them at any time.

"Monica, did you ever drive race cars?" Richard was tugging on the seat belt to make sure it was securely fastened. Her car pitched and leaned when she fought traffic to stay close to the BMW.

"Don't worry, Richard, I've been on some dirt tracks back home that make this drive look like a parade. Back at the academy someone scored second highest in the driving class. Some of the men were a bit testy over that."

"Listen Monica, I only have one life to give. You might be part Calico, but this guy is not a cat.

Richard is shaken by Monica's crafty maneuvering. After a minute, she was back on the terrorist trail. She turns down K Street and then down Michigan Avenue. The Lincoln Town Car is a trifle big in this race. She picks up the terrorist's car rather quickly. Richard didn't think they could keep up. Monica had no desire to give away the fact that she is tracking the terrorists.

The terrorists ended up pulling into a small shopping plaza. As Monica circles the park, Richard keeps an eye on their car. The terrorists pull into a parking spot. They hurry to the front door of a small diner. Richard watches them enter a pizza shop called Mahdi Pizza. Both agent and former bounty hunter turn to each other. The passenger was carrying what looked like a bird cage.

"Mahdi is here too," says an astonished Richard.

15

Finally Home

The FBI bodyguard and bounty hunter left Washington DC after Agent Paula and Monica switched roles. Monica called the Washington bureau. She reported tracking the suspects to a restaurant. The Washington FBI would take the hand-off and post a watch on the pizza shop. Paula, with less experience, was confident she could drive back to Ohio without incident. However, Monica would be close by.

"Richard, you need a change of scenery. You are attracting an enemy that got burned. They know you. At least we think they do. We didn't shake them with our Charlie routine. You are just too hot right now. We are going back to Lake County. We'll use the back roads. You can pick up some personal items at your home but we will leave again. We are going to move a few times. The FBI will buy you photography equipment alone the way. We think equipment like that may aid in our quest to eliminate the bad guys. Our technical group was able to salvage some of your things. The pictures you took of the house that burned down in Buffalo are being analyzed."

"I really need another lap top and a printer, Paula. Do you think the government will fork out a thousand bucks?" he asked.

"Richard, they have a reason to protect you. You are an asset," she said convincingly.

"I'm an ass is more like it. I should never have gotten into the bounty hunting business. Paula, I keep having dreams that come true. Monica was right. I need to join the Salvation Army."

"Your dreams are helping the FBI. As much as we want you to refrain from your bad habit, it does come in handy. If you keep spotting these guys, that is a service to your country. Consider yourself a Minuteman."

"How about that lap top and printer?" Richard begged.

"That's something I'll ask my superior. He might give the OK."

"Since you brought up my habit Paula, I think it would be in our best interest if we stopped at a gas station and fueled up. You need gas and I need to hit the john."

Paula drove down the two lane highway. They came upon a small town convenience store with gas. Richard used the men's room. A tour of the store ended at the checkout. He bought a twelve pack for the road. While he was at the counter, he bought a car air freshener. This measure was needed if Paula protested about the choice of beverage. As an added Ace, he ordered a fancy drink for her. He bought a French vanilla latté. No sooner did he sit in the car he heard the moan.

"Did you have to buy beer?" she asked.

"Hey, I'm a government asset. Think of me as a machine, it needs to be oiled every so often in order to run right. Here, this is for you. It's a French latte."

She looked at him in disgust. That look was familiar; as if it was from one of his ex-wives. Richard didn't want to bring that subject to life. He was content to let her sulk. Just to light her fuse, he popped a tab on a Shorts. This German beer was a favorite of his. He reached in the grocery bag and pulled out the air freshener.

"Here Paula, I hope this will make the trip more enjoyable."

"You still stink, Richard," she said warm-heartedly.

He could see the barrier was removed. Paula loosened up. Richard poured the beer into a soda cup. The twenty ounce cup easily held the can of beer. He opened the car window and pitched the empty can into the trash can. As they sat in the parking lot he polished off two more cans.

"Let's get going," she said.

"One for the road," Richard said.

He was in the mood again. The alcoholic syndrome is in full bloom. He rarely drinks a single beer, always one after another. Richard couldn't stop.

"Where is Monica?" he asked.

"She is close by. We have what you might call close air support."

Paula looked up to the sky and pointed with her finger.

"Monica hired a private airplane to follow overhead. We have an eye in the sky as an added measure of defense. The cell phone tracker system is activated. We will shuffle you around Cuyahoga, Geauga, and Ashtabula Counties until we get a fix on the enemy," she said as she drove West on Route 322.

"We have good reasons to think that some of the al Qaeda members are still planted in Lake County, Ohio. A safe house used by the terrorists was recently exposed. A natural gas explosion at a house in Painesville revealed evidence to substantiate our concern. Investigators found remnants of explosives and weapons."

Richard was working on the fifth can of beer when nature called. He couldn't hold it any longer. He didn't want the restroom calls to be a nuisance.

"Paula, it's time to make a pit stop."

She didn't hesitate. She agreed.

"I'm looking for a respectable place. There's got to be a diner or some bar open at the next town."

Richard figured she needed a pit stop too. He was right but his situation was becoming precarious. His bladder was filled.

"Orwell," she says.

"Home of the great boxers," replied Richard

She pulls into a restaurant parking lot. He makes a sprinters dash to the washroom inside. He saw the pictures of famous boxers who stopped to dine. They didn't stay long. Richard had time to unload the empty beer cans. He had a full cup of beer ready for the last leg of the trip. Orwell wasn't that far from home, another seventy miles and he's home. He didn't last long after they took off. The intoxicated feeling was heavy on his eyelids. He couldn't fend off the sandman. As Richard slept a dream appeared. He saw the vision of their drive from Thompson Township to Chardon, Ohio.

We turned north on Route 528. Paula's cell phone rang. It was Monica on the other end. She had alarming words to deliver.

"Trouble is behind you. You have two speeding cars coming your way. I don't like the way this looks. You better push."

Paula stepped on the accelerator. She turned onto Route 6 using the advantage of a green light.

"They didn't stop at the red light, Paula. This is trouble. I'm calling the OHP," said Monica

"Chardon dispatch, Ohio Highway Patrol, this is an FBI air tracker. Our white Lincoln, an unmarked car, is entering Chardon square.... "

It was midnight. Richard woke up in time to here Paula talking on her cell phone.

"They're gaining on us," she said with an air of concern.

Richard could see Paula was cinching up her seatbelt. She reached into her suit jacket and pulled out her pistol. In a move of expertise, she loaded a round into the chamber. The clicking sound made Richard feel queasy. He thought about the dream as she laid the gun on the console.

"Not this again?" he asked.

"Keep your cool, Mr. Stern. Tighten up your seatbelt. We may have to do some highway tricks. We need to stay fluid," Paula says.

"Paula, trust me, I'm certainly fluid. I have a nice little buzz on right now. I can tell this much. We will be in Chardon and the people will be stopped. The police will be there, not to worry. Another thing, I'm thinking you could pull into the Chardon highway patrol station"

"What I don't want to see is red fluid, you know, the kind that runs in a body."

They passed through the square. A green traffic light turned in their favor. Two Chardon patrol cars were off to the side. They moved across the north end of the square traveling within the speed limit. Paula watched the pursuing cars in her rear view mirror. As the fast moving cars came to the light it changed. The first car couldn't stop properly and rolled through the red light. The patrol cars immediately turned on their flashing lights. The driver of the second car saw enough and braked to a stop. The first car was pulled over. The Chardon police intervened.

"Well, boys, what's the hurry?" asked the neatly dressed sergeant. His partner was at the ready. The Chardon high school teenagers found themselves outnumbered by police. The boys were more surprised by the welcome they received.

"Sorry, sir, I couldn't time the changing light right," said the speedster.

"Son, we have speed limits here. I know you two football players. Use your speed on the football field not the highway. Put this message in your play book. We want to see you boys play a good game next week. Now do this. You take this car for a touchdown and the goal line is at home.

"Yes, sir."

The Chardon officer reported to dispatch.

"Dispatch, the situation is under control. The football players had illegal motion with an automobile. The driver needed a little sportsmanship tune up. No further back up is needed, over and out."

Paula could see the police had the suspects. She reached for her weapon and unloaded the chambered round. She holstered the gun back into her jacket. At that point Richard breathed a great sigh of relief. They passed through town and were heading north on Route 44. She gave Richard thumbs up sign as she talked on her cell phone.

"It's a false alarm, Paula. The people in the two cars were teen-aged boys doing some fast driving. The second car is receiving an inspection by the OHP."

As they pulled into his drive, Richard breathed a sign of relief. Finally the bounty hunter is home. What he needs is a shower and a nap.

"You can rest here tonight, Mr. Stern. Tomorrow we move again."

16

The Used Car Business Plan

Richard indulged in a few evening cocktails at home while finishing up payment of bills that were accumulating from his absence. The neighbor was nice enough to collect the mail while he was away. The last piece of mail was put in the circular file. He was exhausted from all the past adventures. It was time to let the body relax. His snooze lasted an hour as a dream focused attention on an old acquaintance.

The old man from the marina has moved. He was the caretaker at the marina in Fairport Harbor. He relocated back to Parkersburg. Mack is telling the sheriff to be on the lookout for Al Qaeda terrorists.

Richard's dream revealed another al Qaeda operation. He saw a familiar face from one of the old marinas on Grand River. The custodian, Mack, from an up river business was talking as usual. Richard knew Mack from visits to the marina. Mack was the marina operator and sole caretaker of the St. Clair Street marina which was owned by Smitty. Sy Smitty was a retired school teacher, who inherited a run down marina.

Richard wakes up and is flustered by the dream.

"It is true. They are down there. They are in West Virginia. The dreams are real."

He puts his business computer and printer to work. He sends a FAX to the Cleveland, FBI but loses detail as his memory often fails. The message is sent; that is, what he could remember from the dream.

They are buying businesses in this country. The terrorist are moving in cars and trains, going south. I saw marina Mack. Check Parkersburg, West Virginia.

Parkersburg, West Virginia

Mack was happy to be home. He grew up in Parkersburg. Mack was a smooth talker. He always had stories to tell. His maritime adventures could captivate an audience. As a young sailor he visited many lands. While home on leave from the navy he created and nurtured adventure stories to those willing to listen. The stories were too good to simply cast aside. He advanced through a navy career but still maintained contact with the water. His brush with terrorists in Ohio was a premonition of an unlikely meeting in West Virginia. Little did he know more culprits were making a nest in town. Mack, always ready with a fresh story to tell, flaps his jaw bone at the Doe and Nutt's Bakery. He has several patrons and the waitress captivated by his marina tale.

"I was ready for them, terrorists. Al Qaeda, they didn't fool Mack. I gave a full report to the FBI. They relied on my first hand sighting. I was the backbone of their arrests. What I mean is I had first hand knowledge of the terrorists. My keen sense was tuned to a terrorist plot. While I didn't know at first what was being planned neither did the county sheriff. The terrorists came to me looking for a place to stay. They wanted to hire me as their personal custodian. I gave them a place to stay. You see; they set up camp at the marina."

"One young man had a gun. He flashed it at me. I figured he was the bodyguard. He pulled out money as if it was water. He had hundred dollar bills. So much, he almost ripped my shirt stuffing the cash in my pocket. Wads of money to spend and that's what gave them away. Old Mack was ready to take their money. I let the boss know that strangers were in town. Smitty, my boss, was about to get rich. I called Smitty right away to tell him about the new guests. Of course, they weren't really guests. Smitty was shocked when he came to the marina. He got over the shock and took their money.

"Two fellas from the FBI came calling a few months after the terrorist got settled."

Annie Marie Doe, the fourteen year old daughter of Betty Ann Doe, was waiting on the lone customers at the donut shop. She was dressed in white waitress garb with a white apron. The three customers, Snake, Boots Randall, and Corey Calhoun, along with Mack, would be entertainment for Annie Marie. Today it was Mack's show.

"How did you know they were terrorists, Uncle Mack," asked his nephew, Corey, the nineteen year old auto mechanic.

"Listen up, people. Corey, you pay attention to me. I am a trained marina operator. I handle boats and folks. I could see these people didn't have any boats but they had money, big money. One of them flashed a gun and right there I knew I was faced with a split second decision. Are they going to rob me? My responsibility is to oversee the marina operations. I had a marina to protect. My paid up customers had yachts docked at the marina and I had to protect their interests," says the wordy Mack.

"Did they threaten you, Uncle Mack? Were they gonna shoot? How many was there?" asked Corey.

"Oh, they had me outnumbered thirty to one. I gave them a little information about the marina. I said, 'Mister, this marina might be up for sale.'"

"That piece of information got his attention. I then proceeded to negotiate. I was the go-between man. Here is what I mean. I set up the sale of the business to these terrorists. This was part of my business experience. I had the enemy contained. I told the land owner he could cut a deal with these folks. I didn't want to alarm Smitty, the property owner. I was working both sides of the fence. Smitty was on one side and the terrorists on the other. After some serious dealing, I helped both parties cut a deal."

Annie Marie was scrubbing down another table as Police Chief Bernard Langley and Sheriff Pete Vanderland walked into the donut shop. A chorus of greetings was sounded by everyone.

"Hello, folks," said the chief, as the two lawmen took seats by the arm waving Annie Marie. She directed them to the clean table.

"Coffee, chief, coffee, sheriff?" asked Annie Marie.

"That would be fine, Annie Marie," said the chief. Sheriff Vanderland nodded in agreement.

Annie Marie says, "Mack is telling his marina story again. He's a hero, you know. He was part of that big terrorist bust in Ohio. I'm glad he's on our side."

"We know all about it, Annie Marie. Mack is a legend in his own mind," says the chief. The sheriff has a smile on his face as he has also heard second hand accounts of Mack's role in stifling the invaders.

"Mack has celebratory status in this county, Annie Marie. We keep a pock marked picture of him at the shooting range," says the joking Sheriff Vanderland. Everyone has a good laugh at the sheriff's joke.

Mack, not risking any more build up of his story, quickly downs his coffee and says goodbye.

"We've got business to do. You all, take care. Come on, Corey. You need a car that's going to get you to work and back home. We are going to look for a decent car that is dependable. We'll scout a few used car lots today." Mack says as he departs with the young auto mechanic.

"Good deal, Uncle Mack."

Earlier in the Month

Captain Awad is a modern day pirate, a slippery, master organizer of al Qaeda operations. His ability to adapt and conceal insurgent acts keeps him safe. He is a genius outlaw. He concocted the Ohio attack with Mr. Big. The unfortunate adventure in Ohio left some soldiers dead and others locked up, but the botched plan only served to sharpen his desire to undertake another scheme.

Lord Barrie and Captain Awad escape to Washington, D.C. before the FBI could catch them. This is added proof of their uncanny chameleon features. Captain Awad didn't lie low for very long. His insurgent operation is still functioning. More terrorist soldiers are moving into the region. Some are recruited from the Toronto mosque. Because of this infiltration, he is ordered back to Ohio. He passes through Parkersburg W. Virginia to check on a new business that his second in command recommended.

Parkersburg, West Virginia is the site picked by Mr. Mustavi Mahdi, another key al Qaeda leader. He handles the bank lease to locate the next used car business in town. Parkersburg has Route 77 next to it. This main Ohio to West Virginia route will serve the insurgent ring well.

Mr. Mahdi recruits two college age terrorist wannabes as owners to resurrect a used car dealership. Mr. Mahdi moved his lost dealership from Buffalo, New York. His problem is the boys he selected do not have the background or the looks of West Virginians. Captain Awad is quick to point out the problems.

"Mr. Mahdi these two men will be thrown out of West Virginia after one day in the state. They need language polish, southern style, which they certainly lack right now. You need to find Arab hillbillies," decries Captain Awad. This is a bad choice of individuals.

"America is changing, anyone can get into America. Mexican nationals are coming into Ohio all the time. These two men will pass for Mexican immigrants. These two can adapt," says Mr. Mahdi.

"Wash the stripes from the zebra. Is that what you mean?" asks Captain Awad.

Captain Awad paces around and finally agrees to use the two men with an interjection. "See if you can address the issues I have raised. Make these two Muslims into Arab hillbillies."

"Captain Awad, I'm a school teacher. I'll do what I can. I'll advertise a little and see if I can get experienced American salesmen to work the business. Slowly, these two can be worked into the business. In time, they will catch on. If they can imitate college students from Ohio, they should be OK. We have a couple Texas businessmen that run used car businesses in El Paso. Their expertise might work out. Captain Awad, Americans are money hungry. If I wave the right money in their faces they will come."

Later that day Captain Awad talks to his Washington, DC liaison. He explains a way to move troops.

"The prospect of establishing a rest stop and vehicle exchange business in Parkersburg, West Virginia will aid our troop movement. We are establishing a chain of businesses stretching to Texas. You must keep a steady flow of members moving from the Middle East. The Americans haven't protected the northern border yet. Mustavi Mahdi is handling the new business assignment," says Captain Awad over his cell phone.

The Washington call is very encouraging to the terrorist boss. He would like to impress Bin Laden's Washington operatives. He receives operational funds from the Washington, DC embassy.

"Mr. Mahdi and I have labored over personnel issues. We have settled our differences. Send the startup money to the Toledo safe house. I will pick it up," says Captain Awad.

Osama Bin Laden's deputies in Washington, DC would coordinate money laundering. Bin Laden has a few good super cell leaders in Middle America. He did not want to lose any of them. His top man, Mr. Big, has leaders stop in the Nigerian Embassy in Washington, DC every few weeks to exchange ideas. From here, money laundering was not a problem.

Charities operating in mosques continue to do well and send cash.

Opening a business in America was simple. This made disguising a terrorist business most attractive in Mr. Big's quest to rule America. Mr. Big would have Captain Awad pick out used car dealerships and convenience stores along a main route headed south. He would usually pick businesses in pairs. Better if they were located in the same town. This way money and late night traffic is always moving. All illegal activity would appear normal. This plan would keep the cell members secret. Captain Awad mastered-minded this business plan.

Captain Awad made calls to the forgery cell in Detroit. They would create the needed identifications.

"We will need two new identity cards made. Two men will be working in West Virginia." Captain Awad orders two college ID cards. His orders carry considerable weight among the network of cells in North America. He has close ties with Bin Laden. Some primary players in the insurgent ranks know Captain Awad. His organizational skills were often the difference between capture and escape.

"Yes Captain, we will work on this." The lower orderly followed through with the command. The new ID cards were manufactured and shipped from the Detroit mosque.

"I'm happy with my new identity," said Wayne Cartwright. His real name is Moffi el Ahhaf.

"Wayne Cartwright sounds like a West Virginian. After spending a year in Toronto, it is time for new scenery. The last eight month in America was a breeze. Now with our new IDs we can move around the country without question. We will be the next link in the chain to Texas. The Captain will give us a better assignment."

"Adi Habbib is now from West Virginia, not Egypt. I am Matt Q. Olefield," Habbib exclaimed.

"We will learn from Mr. Mahdi. He will teach us the southern customs." Adi Habbib agreed.

Mr. Mahdi worked with the two men to improve their southern style. He did a good job. They moved back and forth though Ohio without difficulty. Hauling cars was part of the routine. Three weeks of non-stop business instruction was building the men's courage. They would stop for brief periods and work at the used car business.

Mr. Mahdi employed a temporary manager for handling paperwork. She didn't ask questions. Her job was taking care of credit and temporary tags.

Mustavi Mahdi still didn't trust the men to maintain control over the business. He worked with them at his convenience store. He taught them at the safe house. Finally, he gave them a black BMW to use. Mr. Mahdi had a job for them. Two cell members would need to be picked up. The men were at the convenience store office and would need to use a van from the used car lot. A shipment of chemicals needed to be moved from the convenience store to a farm in Virginia. These men would do the job.

"Take them from the store and drive to the used car lot. Give them the white van. They will drive to Virginia soon. In the meantime, you two lead them to the safe house. They will stay there until I work out the details of the next move," says Mr. Mahdi.

He didn't want these men getting lost and start driving around in Parkersburg, West Virginia. Mr. Mahdi's regular driver went to Washington, DC for a money transfer. This had Mr. Mahdi worried because he was short-handed. Matt and Wayne were reliable but using them to move chemicals was too risky. They picked up used cars on trips to the Buffalo dealership prior to its closure. They never had a problem driving to Buffalo. Even when they were bodyguards for

Mr. Big, they handled themselves well but Mr. Mahdi preferred to use the older men to deliver the special chemical pellets.

The young terrorists are excited. They have a nice car to drive and a new assignment. This new venture heightens Wayne and Matt's appetite for clandestine work. Providing an escort service is a welcome change in responsibility.

17

FBI Needs a Used Car

The crime fighters did a preliminary check of Parkersburg while they were still in the Cleveland office. They were ready for fishing more than FBI work. Agent Roman always figures in a vacation when away from the office. He has a difficult time believing terrorists are in West Virginia just because Mr. Stern saw them in a dream. In fact, he has a difficult time getting motivated for the assignment.

"Investigating a used car lot probably won't turn up much of anything.

"I've got some nice fishing lures to try, Bill. Fifty bucks says I'll land the biggest trout this weekend."

"That's a bet, buddy. Let's get there early on Saturday, check the recorders office, and start fishing as soon as the sun goes down." Agent Bill Wright replies.

Agent Ron Roman and Bill Wright assembled their fishing equipment. The crime fighters keep fishing equipment in an upright locker in the office. Agent Roman perfects the dual mission approach as he refers to his mixing business with pleasure. This is an exercise they go through each time a new fishing opportunity comes along. Supervisor Moses is sometimes baffled by techniques used by his agents. They get results and for that, he gives them room to research new procedures. He questions the need for both recreation and work at the same time. For Supervisor Moses, results out weigh agency policies.

"The code name for this very special mission is, **FISHING**." Agent Ron Roman recites and prints fishing in large letters on his desk calendar. He traced over the words repeatedly.

"Bill, the West Virginia streams are full of trout. Rainbows, baby, we are going to limit out. The first thing we do is get a fishing license and a trout stamp. We'll use this investigation as our front to go fishing."

"You know, Ron, your priorities are reversed. Cliff thinks we are following up on Mr. Stern's hunch. Oh well, you're not going to fit in with the folks down south anyhow."

"Why is that, good buddy," asked Agent Roman?

"You have the right posture and your full figure is about the right size, but your teeth are too straight and they're white."

"Now that's not very nice, Bill, and that's not very neighborly of you, either. You better get the crackpot jokes out of your system now. You make a comment like that down there and you are liable to be spinning on a barbeque spit."

"If I hook a big one you better be ready with the net," says the anxious Ron Roman.

"Some places down south are still fighting the civil war. I am a northern guy, can I help that?" Bill pleads his case.

Ron switches the subject. He's a little worried about Bill's attitude. Bill received a warning for prejudicial prisoner treatment. That was a few years ago, although Ron believes his partner is careful now and will not go overboard when interrogating prisoners. He got a little physical with a suspected drug pusher, who was an illegal alien of Mexican decent. An internal review board investigated the incident. The Hispanic had a broken arm and nose, which, Bill said, was from a fall.

"It's good to see my top agents at work. Better put some new line on that reel of yours, Ron," comments Supervisor Cliff Moses as he walks through the office.

"We're all business, boss. You know the dynamic duo," says Agent Wright. Cliff Moses shakes his head as he leaves the room. He is well aware of the loose manner in which his agents operate.

"We'll do a sweep of Parkersburg before we get serious about fishing. A new agent is covering the office for us. Did you meet Julie, Julie Suhadolnik?" asked Agent Roman.

"Oh, yeah, I met Julie! She was getting on the elevator and we managed a short conversation. Julie is the jewel. I was going to ask her for a date. You know me, Ron."

"She said she graduated from college a while back and worked for the government on a munitions project with the Army. She said something like that. I can't believe my cupid words wouldn't naturally flow. She caught me off my game. I think we have some commonality." said the handsome Agent Wright.

"Bill, in wrestling they call that a false start. I'll call her later and let her know wolfman Wright is out of the den."

"Hey, pal, I'm an all-American marksmen and all-American ladies man," replies Agent Wright.

"I'll call the Charleston office before we head down and let them know what's happening. They may send a couple of their agents to help out, if we uncover something, but I don't think this will be anything more that a fishing trip on Uncle Sam," says Ron.

Agent Roman places a call to the FBI bureau in Charleston and then orders a rental van.

The following day they head south on route 77. The men have a lap top computer with them and exchange E-mails with the office.

Covering the Cleveland office is Julie. She receives a fax message from Mr. Stern. She immediately sends an Email to Ron and Bill.

'Mr. Stern sent a fax and said the terrorists are in Parkersburg, West Virginia. Terrorists are moving south. Mack is in Parkersburg. I'm not sure if this man is a crackpot but he must know about the Parkersburg investigation. He refers to a West Virginia terrorist cell.'

Agent Wright answers. As he types, he repeats the message to Agent Roman.

'Good morning, Julie, this is Bill Wright. We met on the elevator. Keep us informed about E-mail from Richard Stern. He is a protected witness. We have two agents working with him. This is a complex story. I'll need to have a meeting with you when I get back to cover the detail. Mr. Stern has a history with the Cleveland office. Please be available; just relay any messages to us from Mr. Stern.'

"Hello, Julie, this is FBI Agent Wright, known as wolfman," says the candid Agent Roman. Ron doesn't miss a chance to needle his sidekick. Agent Wright sits comfortably in the passenger seat with the lap top perched atop his knees. He has a sheepish grin on his face after his partner delivers the one line zinger.

"Stern needs another beer. This guy is just taking lucky guesses," says Agent Wright to his partner.

"Mr. Stern said marina Mack is with them? Do you remember the old man at the marina in Fairport Harbor?" asks Agent Roman.

"Stern is talking about Mack McPherson or alias Mack Crenel. He is in Parkersburg," says Agent Wright.

"That old salty sailor from the Lazy Z Marina was from West Virginia. You know, Mack said he has relatives in Parkersburg. Time will tell," adds Agent Wright.

"I looked up used car dealers in the area. A new one just opened. It's called, Good and Fine, used cars. It is located on Hickory Street. It so happens, a river is close by if you know what I mean. We'll start with that one and work around town," Roman says.

18

Mack Meets Al Qaeda

"Just never mind the remarks the sheriff made. Uncle Mack faced the terrorists and the sheriff can't stand the fact. You might just think he's jealous.

"A used car lot just opened on Hickory, Corey. An old junkyard was there years ago before you were born. Since they just opened, for sure they'll be dealing. I'll do the negotiating. You watch Uncle Mack in action. We are parking out of view. If they see my car they might get the wrong impression," says the confident Uncle Mack.

Mack parks his Cadillac on the side of the road, a short distance from the used car lot. Mack didn't want the owner seeing his status symbol.

"This is a great day for car shopping, Uncle Mack. The sun is out. I want the weather to stay nice for the weekend," said Corey

"Everyday is a weekend for me, Corey." Mack is referring to the fact that he's retired now. Mack was married to the sea. He was a merchant marine sailor for twenty-four years. He has plenty of free time to share with Corey now. He missed the boy's early years. Mack didn't have any kids so nephew Corey is a blessing.

Mack devotes time to coach Corey. He understands the struggles his nephew must endure. The boy is branching out, earning a living and making adult decisions. Mama was in her thirties when Corey was born. Corey's mama is housebound now. She suffered a stroke that left her partially crippled. Mack is attempting to change the family's luck.

Corey spots a yellow Z-28 parked near two other Chevy cars.

"Take a look at this baby, Uncle Mack," suggests Corey.

"That is a sharp car, Corey but you'll burn the tire off that car. You'll have that flipped over or down in a hollow in a week. Let me be the guide today, Corey. I'm here as a guide and I'll offer advice. Don't make any hasty decisions."

The two men filed past other cars as the sales clerk comes out to introduce himself.

"I'm Maffi, oh, my nickname, sorry. I'm. I am Wayne, Wayne Cartwright, your used car salesman. The boss isn't here right now so you might pick out a car now and get a good, the best deal," says Mr. Cartwright.

Cartwright almost slipped up. The young man's comments were not very sharp. His speech wasn't fluid. He seemed unsure of himself. Mack was alert to this fact. The man's sales pitch was weak. His performance needs work. Mack's quick assessment of young Cartwright's demeanor suggested the man was a newcomer to the business.

"You're new at this business, young man. Be assertive." Mack was doing some coaching; trying to help the young sales rep.

"Are you just starting?" asked Mack.

"I have experience," said Mr. Cartwright. Mack wasn't about to believe that.

Corey asks, "Which cars are the best deals?"

"I'm looking and thinking about buying now. I have a better job. I'm saving money for a good used car," says Corey.

"All of our vehicles are well equipped and the price is on the windshield. We try to stock cars that have less than fifty thousand odometer miles. Our boss is out of town now, buying more low mileage cars. He will be here tomorrow."

"In that case we'll be back tomorrow to see the boss and the new low mileage cars. Old Mack needs time to think about what we saw today. You need a little work on your delivery, son," says Mack.

"We'll be back," says Corey.

"Uncle Mack, why are we leaving so soon?" asks Corey.

"Corey, if the boss isn't here, we won't get a deal. We'll check back here. Bring five hundred bucks with you tomorrow."

The early morning sun is just about to appear on the horizon. The two FBI agents leave from Cleveland at midnight. They stop at a rest area for about an hour to freshen up after driving most of the night. The two crime fighters drive into Parkersburg city limits and use the Map Quest locater to find Hickory Street. It didn't take long to find the used car business. The closed business is an old brick building. On the side of the building is a weight scale used years ago to weigh scrap metal. Bill and Ron drive by the office, eagle-eyeing the layout. They do a cursory check before anyone arrives. The lot has about twenty-five cars parked on it. Yellow barrels mark the dead end street. Beyond the barrels the river forms a border almost semi-circling the parking lot. The land surrounding the river is wooded, offering a pristine environment for hunting and fishing. The agents stop at the dead end to admire God's nature.

"Look at this river, Bill. The trout are ready to jump in the van. We'll try our hand at fishing later today. We saw enough of this place. We'll stop back here and work a little undercover surveillance near the river if you know what I mean. We need to find a bait shop."

Later that day, Corey spots two trailers of used cars pass the auto repair shop where he works. He makes a quick judgment of the cars.

"I just know those cars are going to the Good and Fine used car dealership!" He exclaims.

While on lunch break, Corey calls Uncle Mack.

"I think the used cars that salesman talked about are in town, Uncle Mack. When I get off work, let's go back to that Good and Fine used car lot and see if those cars are going there."

"OK, Corey, I'll pick you up. I'll outsmart that young guy. If the boss is there, we'll talk to him first and see what cars are new on the lot. You just watch old Uncle Mack work a deal."

They arrived at the used car lot near closing time. Mack parks his caddie out of view as he did before. Corey, thrilled by the thought of buying a better set of wheels, hurries to the lead.

With Uncle Mack's financial help, the prospect of a low car payment was definitely a possibility. Both men round an outgrowth of bushes and cross a mud trail leading to the river. A line of bushes separates the lot from the trail. A black car passes Mack and Corey then pulls into the used car lot.

Corey races ahead of Mack. Corey's fast pace reminded Mack of his first car experience. Mack's legs suddenly gained some youthful spring. The fun of shopping for a used car kindles a warm feeling for him. That atmosphere cools, then slams shut as Mack becomes not a used car buyer, but a witness. Approaching the BMW, Mack looks inside the car from a short distance. A passenger sits with a returning stare. It is someone Mack remembers. The smoky glass window obscures a perfect vision of the man's face. Enough facial features are captured. Mack makes a fist. Tension grips his body. A legion of goose bumps crawl along the retired sailor's arms, even though the weather is warm.

Released from memory is a photo of a terrorist. The shock is a lightning snapshot. Almost a year to the day an image of a terrorist was burned into his head. Before Mack is the terrorist bodyguard, who greeted him at the Lazy Z, marina. At the time, the man issued a warning by presenting a pistol for Mack to view. Mack understood the threat. His memory paid an unwelcome reminder, shattering the car hunt.

"Corey, we need to wait. Corey, stop," pleads Mack.

Corey couldn't turn back. He hurried into the office. Mack is waving his arm as a gesture to come back. Corey, oblivious to his Uncle's recall, enters the office. Once inside, he walks to the occupied desk and stands at attention.

The phone rings as Mack enters the office. Corey's hearing is still blocked by anticipation. Mack, on the other hand, is calculating the next step. Looking for another exit, Mack searches the office with his eyes. A back door is closed and the hall leading to it is littered with cleaning supplies.

The man on the phone holds up one finger. The implied expression is to wait one minute. Behind Mack, the door opens and a trench coated man orders the men outside.

"Gentlemen, follow me. Come outside."

Uncle Mack grabs Corey by the arm.

"How about letting me use your phone, mister?" asks Uncle Mack.

"We are closed," says the manager at the desk as he hangs up the phone.

"Folks, you made a mistake coming here. We have another car lot not far from here. My associate will show you the way," replies the man behind the desk.

19

Fishing for Terrorists

The agents rode around town checking for a bait shop that would be open so early in the morning. It wasn't long before they found one. The fishing and hunting store even rented all terrain vehicles. The owner said they could drive the ATV to the Little Kanawha River from the store. What was even better, they could leave their van at the store as the used car lot on Hickory wasn't far away.

"You boys picked a good spot for bass and trout. Start fishing the river behind that old converted junk yard," said the bait shop owner.

"We sure hope so. Thanks a bunch, sir, we appreciate your business. We'll start fishing later today. First we need to drop off our luggage at the motel," says Roman.

The motel selected was on the south side of town. The motel room had a shower, color TV and two single beds. What was convenient was the short drive to the bait shop. The two agents did some detective work after unpacking and then made a visit to the auditor's office.

After checking county records, they discovered the parcel of land the used car lot sits on is owned by a Parkersburg bank. The two agents pay a visit to the local bank. The bank president speaks vaguely about the arrangement the bank has with the lessee. What they do find out is that the bank has leased the property to a Detroit, Michigan, business. The business is listed as Mahdi Enterprises.

A phone call to the FBI Headquarters in Washington, DC verifies the names of Mahdi businesses and a charitable agency. Seven Mahdi brothers are partners along with an Iraqi politician, a lawyer from Washington State, and a Nigerian embassy staffer. Three of the brothers are executives with a charitable organization call the Group Unity of Nigeria. Group Unity of Nigeria has a mosque in Detroit and Toronto, Canada.

"G.U.N. is in Canada too, very interesting. The charitable Mahdi brothers might be tied to al Qaeda," Roman said.

"This is looking more and more like trouble than any charity group. We have one of the Mahdi brothers locked up. He was the store owner in the Ohio plot. Wasn't he called bird man, Ron? He had a talking bird," Agent Wright says.

"Yeah, I remember. Let's get moving. We are in West Virginia fishing and hunting country. We'll check the used car lot next."

The agents return to the bait store and transfer fishing equipment to the ATV. Ron Roman drives the ATV to start the fishing adventure. As they drive on the side of the paved road, the mood changes. FBI business becomes a matter of fact. The agents start checking ammunition.

The used car lot is about half mile away. The agents aren't talking. This lack of communication triggers an air of anxiety. Bill Wright adjusts his holstered service pistol to accommodate the fishing vest. Ron feels for his weapon almost anticipating trouble. Their preliminary investigative work turned up more than they expected. Mahdi brothers are in Parkersburg, West Virginia. The color of the investigation has turned orange for what could be suspicious activity. This is not what the agents anticipated. Most of the information is circumstantial but it all fits. Terrorist activity is definitely a possibility. Fishing and detective work usually blend well for the agents. This time, the agent's fishing trip is getting a nibble and it isn't fish.

As their ATV nears the used car lot, a white van is pulling out from the lot's drive. The van is dented and dirty. The driver appears to be wearing a gown and a head dress.

"I don't believe this," Agent Wright exclaims! Ron slows down to get a good look at the van. The tinted windows of the van do the job, hiding the faces of the occupants.

"What do you think, Ron? Are we profiling or is that an Arabian person?"

"We can't assume anything at this point," claims Roman.

"We are almost in their back yard. They don't have many cars on the lot," says Agent Wright, while trying to avoid assuming the van is suspicious.

Agent Wright, well noted for his reactive style, checks his reserve pistol tucked against his inside calf muscle.

"You always do that, Bill, and it means trouble," growls Agent Roman.

"Do what, Ron," asks Agent Wright?

"You know. You know what you're doing."

Agent Roman is quite accustomed to his partner's antics. They have been in skirmishes and Bill often takes command. Ron is usually at the tail end of trouble as Agent Wright is nimble and fleet footed.

"Do what Ron?"

"You keep the second pistol hidden. Then you feel for it. The next thing I see and hear is bang, bang, bang. You empty the Glock. Then you're pulling out the second pistol. I know you, Bill."

"Please, please don't say anything, no provoking, no shooting, no nothing! We are observers. There is that look on your face. Bill, you have a low flash point, like gasoline."

Bill shakes his head. So slight is the OK that it isn't reassuring. Roman knows his partner is an expert target shooter. His hand and eye coordination are unmatched by anyone in the bureau.

The mood is somber. Bill transfers two ammo clips to his vest pocket. They both watch intently. The front passenger door opens and a big man exits the car. He is wearing a dark trench coat and a skull cap covers his head. The big man turns to look at the ATV. They pass within thirty yards of the van.

"Don't look at him, Bill."

"He's Middle Eastern."

"No, he isn't. Forget it, Bill. You don't know that."

Agent Roman is visibly upset. He wants to observe the situation nonchalantly. Deep down, they both assume the worst. The sacred part of America may have terrorist cells. Richard Stern may be right. They pass the office and drive to the back of the property. When they approach the river, both men calm down. The noise of the water quells the tension of the past few minutes. The serenity of the river relieves the strain. The men calm down.

The Little Kanawha River is within twenty yards of the back property line. The used car lot has a brick rim that lines the back of the car lot. It's about two feet high and used to keep water from entering the lot when heavy rains swell the river. Ron parks the ATV directly behind the wall where they can see most of the used cars.

The white van leaves and then a black sedan parks in the same place. It parks along the side of the office building facing the back of the used car lot.

Ron is busy unpacking his fishing gear. He has a favorite pole ready to go.

"I forgot about these. These are John West lures. Ever heard of them, Bill? I got them about a year ago from a guy by the name of Hucks. He was fishing nearby on the Grand River in Fairport Harbor. He said try these lures. He handed two of them to try but it was time to leave and I never did get to use them. Now is the time to test them," says the upbeat Ron Roman.

Agent Roman is so excited about fishing in West Virginia that he bravely volunteers to fish first. He's not ready to start the stakeout but he is ready to catch the first rainbow. On the other hand Bill prefers to start the stakeout. The agents have both an ideal place to keep an eye on the used car lot and fish the Little Kanawha River.

"Go ahead and start fishing, Ron. I'll keep a lookout for the first hour. We'll do a time-share stakeout. You do the fishing for now."

"Maybe we jumped the gun back there by assuming the worst," adds Bill.

"That's what I think, Bill. We just need to settle down."

Agent Wright pulls out a camera that is wrapped in a towel. He attaches a long range lens on it. He tosses a sleeping bag to the ground. He locates and removes binoculars from a duffle bag. After clearing an area behind the brick wall, he unfolds the sleeping bag and sits down. He takes a practice picture of Ron lumbering down the side of the dirt bank.

Agent Wright uses the ATV to provide a comfortable position with his back against the door. The agent has a clear view of the black sedan. A little bit of brush and weeds provide cover to conceal the lookout station. The agents aren't far from the used car office. Bill guesses the distance to be one hundred yards away.

Agent Roman makes his way down the bank to the river. He is all fishermen and begins casting the home made lure into the stream. In seconds he hooks a trout and nets the fish. He quickly puts it on a stringer. He catches three more and releases them. They are a little too small for the stringer. Agent Roman is having a great time. He doesn't bother to tell his buddy the fishing is outstanding. He wants to win the fifty buck bet. The evening fishing is better than the bait shop people reported. About fifteen minutes go by before he hooks a big fish. His light weight line is pressured almost to the breaking point. It is an angler's dream come true, as he fights to land the fish. In his haste to start fishing, he forgot to bring a net with him.

"Bill, I got a big one hooked. You better get the net." A row of saplings block the view and muzzles the sound of Agent Roman. As he battles the trout, he doesn't realize Bill can't see or hear him. The fish pulls him further away from the stakeout.

Bill adjusts the focus on the camera. He watches two men walk to the office of the used car lot. The driver and one passenger get out and walk to the side door of the office. The one man stops to look around. He has a hand gun visible. The trench coated man enters the office, following the other people. Someone inside the car opens the back door of the sedan. After a minute people start filing out of the used car office. As they step outside, the man in the trench coat has a gun drawn. The two customers have their hands raised.

Agent Wright zooms in on one of the customers.

"Ron, I think Marina Mack is at the used car lot. It sure looks like him and it looks like trouble," says Agent Wright. He speaks, but not loud enough for Ron to hear.

Bill operates the focus and zoom lens on the camera again and again. He wants to get a picture of the people around the black sedan. He snaps a picture and grabs the binoculars because he notices an agitated Mack. Something has caused Mack to get excited. He appears to be yelling at the passenger in the black sedan.

"Something is definitely wrong, Ron, come up here." Bill voices his concern but the sound isn't loud enough for Agent Roman to hear. Agent Wright doesn't wish to give away his position by speaking louder.

The man inside the black sedan is now outside. He pulls out a hand gun and has Mack and the other person walk over to the car and they get into the back seat of the car. Bill watches intently. Precious seconds tick away as another terrorist exits the other side door of the car.

Agent Wright sets the binoculars down and springs into action. He starts to run through the bushes next to the used car lot. The bushes act to shield him. This prevents the two men standing by the BMW from seeing him approach. Within twenty-five seconds he is close to the men.

"FBI. Drop your weapons," orders the agent.

The terrorists are surprised. They lurch and try to take aim at the agent. A rapid fire is released by Agent Wright striking one and then the other terrorist. The first man is hit twice in the chest sending him flying across the front of the BMW. His associate is struck in the midsection and doubles over. Another bullet hits him again. This time, it finds the top of his head, killing him instantly. The door to the office opens and two trench coated men stand side by side trying to aim their guns at the shifting and weaving agent. Agent Wright uses the BMW effectively, shielding his body. He moves to the back side wall and throws a rattle fishing lure on the ground. The sound of the rattle is a magnet for the terrorist's gunfire. Instinctively, Agent Wright pops from the front of the car. The two terrorist are openly visible. Agent Wright has no chance to exchange greetings. He surprises the terrorists and fires four successive shots. The first man is hit, spins, and slams against the office door breaking the glass. A second shot hits him in the back sending him through the door. The other man is cut down. He hits the weight scale with a flying sit motion. His handgun does a few cartwheels across the parking lot signaling his last criminal act is over. His body is sitting up as if waiting to be weighed.

Mack points his finger across Corey at the door, signaling an exit strategy. Corey bolts from the back door, Mack dives out the other side of the BMW.

"Terrorist in the car!" Mack yells.

The terrorist in the front seat slides over and starts the car. As he pulls away, he veers toward the diving Agent Wright. The agent rolls clear of the on coming tire and fires point blank into the front passenger door and window. The side-arm motion causes a vector pattern of bullet holes on the door. An air bag is deployed and the car ploughs into another parked car. The wreckage showers the ground with broken glass.

Agent Roman hearing the sound of gunshots yells.

"Fish is hooked, Bill. What's going on?" Listening and hearing nothing but more gun shots, Agent Roman immediately sets down the rod and lumbers up the bank. His large hulking frame battles to climb up the bank. He is cursing silently as he plows ahead.

"Jesus Christ, forgive my partner. Don't tell me, dear God, I already know. Christ, Bill, not now. Bad timing, Bill. I've got a big one on the line and off you go. I knew it. He touches that calf pistol and it means trouble. Damn it, Bill," whispers Agent Roman.

The commotion settles. Agent Roman climbs over the parking lot barrier only to see a man hiding behind a parked car about fifteen yards away. The man is crouched down facing the office. He has a hand gun in his right hand. Agent Roman pulls his weapon from the holster.

Agent Roman moves slowly. Cautious as he is, the parking lot has debris scattered throughout. He passes between two cars. His silent creep ends as he steps on a small twig which snaps. The sound, while slight is like a game ending horn going off. The man is alerted and turns.

"FBI, drop the gun." The man points his hand gun toward the big agent. The exchange of gun fire lasts for three shots. Agent Roman moves toward the fallen man.

He is hit in the upper chest. Agent Roman checks for the man's pulse and then removes the man's wallet. He removes his college ID card.

"Wayne Cartwright, you are under arrest." The agent reads the dead man his rights.

"You have the right to die a slow death but I'm a good shot," says Agent Roman.

Across the street is Mrs. Jenny McAlpine. She watched most of the fireworks from her picture window. Her hands still cover her mouth. Recovering from the shock, she yells to her son.

"Call the sheriff!"

Ambulance, police, and Sheriff Pete Vanderland arrive to sort through the casualties and record the investigation.

"You're late, sheriff," says Uncle Mack. A bandage covers a head wound on Mack's head. Corey and Mack are talking to Agent Wright and Roman.

"We got um, sheriff. Corey and Uncle Mack are helping the FBI round up this garbage." Corey hugs his Uncle.

Agent Roman turns to his partner.

"Hold down the fort, Bill, you interrupted an important part of this trip."

"Where are you going, Ron?"

"Fishing, I'll be back."

Agent Roman jogs back to check his fishing rod. He lifts the rod and feels for the trout that he had hooked.

"I lost a big one," says Roman.

Back at the bait shop, the agents return the ATV. At the same time a young boy about twelve years old is at the counter checking in a magnificent catch. Fishermen are huddled around the boy, admiring a record trout he caught. The boy said his fishing line tangled with another line and he landed the monster trout. The boy's rainbow trout is on the counter. It has a lure hanging from the lip. There, for everyone to see is the John West lure. Agent Roman and Wright look at each other after observing the fish.

Roman's face turns fire engine red, but he maintains a closed mouth. Laughing under his breath is Agent Wright. He puts a hand on his partner's shoulder and quips.

"Hey, Ron, that boy uses a John West lure just like yours."

20

The Shell Game

Richard needed to check his house for any problems after being away for weeks. A shower was the first order of business. Being home and taking a warm shower relaxed his body. Staying awake after his first shower in three days was a chore. The cleansing sensation of the shower was uplifting, although another matter was in the back of his mind. He wondered. "Is the FBI really shielding me from danger?"

This self-doubting thought was a sign of a breakdown. The accumulated effects of alcohol abuse impaired his judgment. He was in need of total abstinence. With all the trouble, travel, and worries about the future, his mental condition was deflating. A measure of his own state came from the hallucination of the Erie Indian. At this point Richard reasoned correctly, he was way beyond normal recreational use.

Richard checked his phone messages. One of them was from the mayor. Good old Mayor Reese Conway was campaigning for election. He was a shoe-in for another term. The mayor and his cronies were playing a shell game. It was called hide the truth about the terrorist. If you listen to him, he single handedly arrested most of the terrorists. While Mr. Big duped him into thinking a great renaissance was coming, Mayor Reese managed to change the events in his favor. Grant Michell did the same in Grand River. They both proclaimed their leadership role led to the roundup of al Qaeda members. They concurred to create a common story that they enticed the terrorists into a trap. Because of their secret deals most people didn't have a clue or didn't care what was going on at city hall. They used this air of secrecy to give the impression they were working with the FBI to foil the terrorist plan. To a degree that was true, except the FBI was checking into city hall's collaboration with the enemy.

Fairport Harbor's annexed property was under development by Barrie the Lion Builders. The builder abandoned the annexed property when the terrorist plot was foiled. The developer Lord Barrie, a terrorist himself, escaped with Mr. Big and Captain Awad.

Mayor Conway staked political capital on the improvement project. After the terrorist plot was foiled, the mayor was rescued by a new developer with ties to a Columbus, Ohio bank. Grand River and Painesville all shared in a new development plan. This was another political win for Mayor Conway. In Richard's view, Reese was a skilled mayor. He was expanding Fairport's tax base. The port authority had a little egg on their face. They managed to deflect criticism. Salvador Cambello, the Fairport Harbor Port Authority treasurer, used his money shifting ability to finance a marina project. This maneuver stifled residences' criticism. He earned a new title. Sal is proclaimed a maverick when handling money. Enough money was parleyed from private donation to win additional capital grants. The port authority bilked the terrorists out of thousands for supplies never used. Advance payments, made to Sal Cambello for the courtesy docks, was another wind-fall the terrorists left behind.

Another victory was achieved by the Lake County Commissioners when they moved to establish a county port authority. This was one of Richard Stern's major goals. He brought attention to the fact that the county could reap a return if it created a county port authority. It took four and a half years to accomplish but everyone earned a degree of satisfaction. The county would be in better position to finance capital projects and port security will receive far more attention.

The Fairport Harbor Coast Guard was provided a new patrol boat armed with additional fire power. Coast guard security procedures were improved. A new fence was installed around the coast guard station along with port security cameras. A Lake Erie patrol was assigned a greater role. Greater emphasis was placed on boat inspections. The coast guard was alert for unusual freighter port calls. Ship inspections would be the rule and carried out as deemed necessary. Port security was beefed up around the station. Even area industry improved security measures throughout the county.

The first night passed without a problem. Supervisor Moses made the decision to pause at Richard's home before moving along. He discussed a plan to move Richard to a Cuyahoga County safe house with Paula and Monica but favored chess moves. He didn't want them staying in one place day after day. Moses had options because of Monica's expertise. She could set traps and operate undercover stings. The thought of using Richard Stern as shark's bait to capture terrorists crossed his mind. Both agents had Marshall Art's skills and could humble people twice their size. They did not lack physical agility. This was the main reason he kept them working the protection assignment.

Cliff Moses instructed the lady agents to move Richard back and forth. Show him in his daily routine once. Then we move him again. He will have another agent switch cars with them as an added measure of security. They will make a switch in Grand River at Perchmans Restaurant.

"Be at the restaurant around nine o'clock, Paula. Julie will make the switch with you. Also, I want all of you to be on your toes. The enemy has suffered more losses. Almost as a fore warning, he adds words of caution. This is a time when both sides make mistakes," Moses warns.

Before Paula and Richard leave town they stopped at the neighborhood clubs. Richard wanted to say hello and goodbye at the same time. This was a ritual of his. Prior to any trip out of town, he would stop at the local watering holes. Most clubs keep a member coming back by offering a contest to win cash. If a person stops to sign up for the cash prize, you could win. A drawing is held each night. Richard wanted to be included in that day's drawing. This was more or less an excuse to have another drink. Richard was surprised Paula didn't protest when he told her he needed to sign the book at the local clubs. She had a reason for that.

"We have a new plan that you shall see. A wire tap will be on your phone. Incidentally, if anyone should ask, I'm your niece from California. My name is Tamara Sake. Tammy is my nickname. That shouldn't be too hard for you to remember Uncle Richard. Just think of the Japanese drink. I'm here on business. You are driving me around showing me the town attractions."

Paula followed Richard into the club. Richard knew she would attract attention. She was young and beautiful and these love-starved drinkers would get a rise out of seeing an older man escorting a young lady.

The local club, called the Honey Hole, is a local tavern designed to help preserve the Ottoman culture. It is a stopping point for thirsty members. Horst Beamer, the town administrator, uses the bar with regularity. His European upbringing fits nicely in the club. He brings to the club his heritage and knowledge of many countries surrounding the Mediterranean Sea. Richard spots Horst sitting on a bar stool, perched there, like a lighthouse beacon. The gravitational pull of spirits keeps Beamer coming back to the club every day, right after work. This day was no different. For Richard, the Honey Hole offers a thrifty price on all beverages.

"Horst, I'm back from New York. I was shooting sports pictures for a national magazine in Syracuse, New York. Actually, they were going to take shots at me but Tamara's friend Monica took over. That's a little inside joke. This national sports magazine's content is for coaches and sports officials. I hope they can use some of my work. My New York travel was very explosive. You could almost say

I was on the receiving end of a big bang. I was really on the go." Richard candidly compressed the truth.

"Oh, forgive me, Horst, I'd like you to meet my niece, Miss Tamara Sake. Call her Tammy as many folks do. She helped me in New York and decided to follow me home. Tammy is a travel agent. This girl is really helpful if your travel plans ever start to explode. I'm heading out again. I may be gone a couple of days or a week. Work is causing me to be a moving target. The next photo ops will take me out West."

"Hello, Miss Tammy. It is a pleasure to meet such a beautiful girl. Your choice of company may be in question," said Horst.

"Richard, did you have trouble on your journey to Syracuse, New York?" asked Horst.

As Horst Beamer was about to speak, his cell phone beeped. Horst reached into his pocket and extracted the cell phone. Horst cupped the phone in his hand to prevent anyone from seeing the message.

"Pardon the message; business is good for you, Richard. It is good to see you. Your photo business must be going well. Thing are starting to die down around here. Pardon me for a moment," said Horst. Richard knew Horst had a little bit of the mayor's Pinocchio antics in him. Horst steps away and uses his cell phone in private.

When he returns he picks up the conversation.

"Business calls are trouble but they pay the bills," says Horst.

"That's what it is all about, Horst," said Richard.

"Bartender, bring a couple beers for Horst and I," commands Richard.

"Tamara, would you like a drink," asked Richard?

"No thanks, Uncle Richard. I'm fine."

"Horst, have a shot of blackberry brandy and then off we go. Tamara is doing the driving."

With that, Richard ordered two shots and paid his tab. Horst and Richard saluted each other as they hoisted the shots. Their brief conversation was interrupted again by Horst Beamer's cell phone.

Richard said adios. It was time to leave before he loses control. As it turns out, Paula and Richard took off just in time. Richard was starting to get comfortable. They stopped at the local VFW and departed for Cleveland.

Paula drove to the Mentor mall using Route 84. They stopped at an electronics store and bought a lap top computer and a printer. He could write a story as the shell game developed. Paula told Richard that Monica would be staying at his house and would join them soon.

"Why is she staying at my house?" Richard asked.

"We have a plan that might expose the terrorists. If the terrorists are around, they may pay a visit. On the other hand if someone in town is an accomplice, that person might pay a visit. In either case we might gain information that will lead us to more terrorists. Monica is there to intercept any phone calls or messengers. She will be checking to see if anyone tries to get into your home. By showing you off today, we will find out if the bad guys know you and if they know where you live. Fairport Harbor is a small town. Any stranger in town will stick out. We know these people. They might try to take you out if they know your location. To be on the safe side our supervisor wants us to keep moving you around. We want to keep you safe. By using you as a decoy today we will find out what we need to do next. Remember, they lost a soldier near Syracuse. They don't want to get caught. You can say we have placed nuts on the ground. We will see if the squirrel shows up. To say it another way, fighting terrorists is a shell game and we are ready to crack some nuts."

Richard knew Paula was serious. She didn't stutter a bit as she talked. He could see the fire in her eyes. Richard could only assume that these two lady agents weren't afraid to confront the enemy.

21

Visitors

It was almost nine o'clock in the evening. After shopping at the Mentor mall, Paula and Richard changed direction. They came back to the neighboring town and stopped for dinner at Perchmans Restaurant in Grand River. The restaurant, known for the best French fries around the area, was also used to exchange cars.

Richard got into a discussion about the daily routine of a detective. The questions started to bombard Paula.

"How do you decide who is going to be working in surveillance? How many agents are actually watching during a stakeout? Does Monica work alone? If Monica is at my house and you are with me, doesn't she need a partner?" asked Richard.

Richard had plenty of questions for Paula. He wanted to be a bounty hunter again in spite of the danger. He believes the bounty hunting adventure allowed him to be with two beautiful agents. Most men would sell their souls to have two ladies become personal escorts. His crash course in detective work came first hand from Paula. He picked her brain and found out the errors in the way he snooped. Since the FBI wants to keep tabs on him, he may as well learn from experts.

"If I would be staying in my house tonight, my .22 magnum pistol would be at my side. That is, of course, if I could load it without shooting myself."

"Loading your pistol is a starter, but you can forget about guns while you are with me, Mr. Stern," says Paula.

Another agent, Julie Suhadolnik, enters the restaurant and nonchalantly passes Paula, handing her a set of keys. At the same time she points out back and walks away.

"Let's leave now. Use the back door; we are switching cars."

Richard and Paula exit the restaurant and leave in the new car. She explains more detail as they drive to another location.

"We are going to stay at a hotel for the night. The FBI is putting you up at a fancy Wickliffe hotel tonight. We are going to be moving you around. There are many investigations going on all over. We don't want you in one place for very long and we are short on manpower right now. You might say things are getting hot in the kitchen and our boss is being extra careful right now."

"Are we sharing a room?" asked Mr. Stern.

"Yes, and you are sleeping on the floor," quips Paula.

Back at Richard Stern's house, Monica is busy.

Monica rearranged the furniture in the living room to her liking. She inflates the doll called Charlie and sits him in a chair near the window. She has the blow up mannequin sitting with a book on his lap. She turns the lights off in the room. A slight bit of street light shines on the mannequin.

The vibrate mode on her cell phone alerts her to retrieve a phone call.

"Hello, Monica, how's it going?" asks Paula.

"Hold on, Paula, Richard's home phone is ringing."

"Richard, Monica says your home phone is ringing. Maybe some hot babe is calling you," Paula gestures to Richard with her finger to move closer.

"Paula, somebody pulled into the driveway," whispers Monica.

Paula is straining to listen to Monica.

Monica grabs the phone but doesn't pick it up. She watches the message on the phone's caller ID.

"The caller ID says, unknown caller and data lost." She talks softly as she looks out the window.

"Monica heard a car pull into your drive," says Paula.

A car door opens, squeaks, and slams.

"Someone is getting out of the car," says Monica

Monica prepares to intervene if the person is the enemy. Her gun is drawn. It is eleven-thirty at night. The noise from the car door would make an assassination or intruder unlikely. Monica darts into the family room. She moves over to the window to have a look. The house lights are off. The window shades keep most of the street light from shining inside the family room. There is a small opening which permits Monica enough visibility to monitor outside activity. The person in the driveway walks up to the window almost at the point where Monica is standing. His frame is a silhouette against the window shade.

Tap, tap, tap, the person is gently rapping on the window. The person walks to the front door. He pushes the plunger on the door handle. The screen door opens and then the handle on the main door starts to turn.

Monica whispers to Paula, "I thought the door was locked."

The unknown man walks right in as if invited. He is standing in a small entrance way separating the family room from the living room.

Monica can't believe she left the door unlocked. Monica is behind a door only a few feet from the intruder. The unidentified man can't see her because the door between the two rooms is closed. The family room is spacious. Monica looks at a door that exits to the garage. She could use this door to escape but the garage door is closed.

The mystery person climbs three steps and enters the nearly dark living room. Monica whispers the sequence of events to Paula as they unfold. She is mystified by the brazen manner of this man. Monica opens the door slightly to watch what the man is doing. She senses the aroma of smoke and beer. She hears his deep breathes, indicating a person that is physically out of shape. The intruder has obviously been drinking and smoking. He moves to a couch near the mannequin.

"Richard, it's Horst Beamer, you didn't leave town. Sorry for the late visit, are you sleeping? If you don't mind, time for me to rest, too much Honey Hole," he says.

The drunken village administrator collapses on the couch.

"He's talking to Charlie. His name is Horst Beamer. He thinks our blowup doll is Mr. Stern," Monica reports.

"He's obviously very drunk. The smell of booze is overwhelming. I'm going to let him rest."

Monica is quite pleased with the way she arranged the dummy.

"The dummy is talking to the dummy," she says trying not to laugh.

It didn't take long for Horst to fall asleep. Monica creeps over to the mannequin, all the while keeping an eye on Horst Beamer. She quietly removes the Charlie doll.

"He won't pose a problem if he stays this way. Tell Mr. Stern his friend came over. Horst Beamer is visiting."

Paula is getting a good laugh out of the situation.

"I know Monica is laughing now, but I think she was a little up tight. Mr. Stern, your friend, Horst Beamer, came over to visit. Isn't he a nice guy?" asks Paula.

"Why would Horst Beamer come to my house? Something is not right. You better tell Monica to watch out."

"Monica, I met Horst Beamer today at a Fairport bar. Richard says he is not a close friend. You better stay alert."

"Ask Monica for the reason he is in my house," commands Richard.

"Richard wants to know something. Why is Horst Beamer at his house?" asks Paula.

"Paula, he is drunk. What do I know?" Monica answers.

Horst Beamer starts to mumble in his sleep. "Stop, Mahdi,"

22

What Happened to Horst?

It was very early in the morning. A vibration in Horst's pocket was his wakeup call. Horst Beamer wakes up from his drunken stupor and looks around, unable at first to decipher what is happening. The cell phone vibrates again, giving Horst another chance to come back to reality. His mind is like a hot shower room mirror. The effects of the booze are still in his system. He sits up feeling his pants pockets for keys and the phone. The window offers him a chance to figure out where he is.

Now mindful of the fact that the house where he woke up is not his, he makes a fast exit. Relieved that the car keys are in his pocket and his car is parked in the drive, Horst Beamer hops in and heads for home.

Monica keeps an eye on him as he leaves the drive. She is both relieved and concerned about his drunken words. The FBI is building a file of data from key names. Mahdi is like saying, 'fire,' in a theater. Nationally, FBI agents pay attention to the Mahdi name, because al Qaeda terrorists are sure to be connected.

Horst Beamer glances at the cell phone message as he drives down East Street. The message on the phone is from a superior.

"You are late. More visitors are coming. Look behind you. Pull over at the park."

A car flashes the headlights behind Horst's car. The rear view mirror has a set of headlights shining on it half blinding Horst as he looks to see who it is. The black sedan only has one person inside. Horst can see him as he turns left onto Plum Street and pulls his car over to park. The car behind does the same. Both cars are parked next to the World War II cannon stationed at Veteran's Park.

Horst pushes down on the button that powers his window. As the window glides down, he looks straight ahead only shifting his eyes to the side mirror. He is afraid his beer breath will tip off the person that he's still under the influence. Horst is trying to do two things at once. His shaky hands don't do him any favors as he fusses with the cell phone. He's advancing through the messages that he missed and watches the car behind him. A bearded man steps outside from his car as another black sedan passes. The man walks up to his car. He has a slight limp. The other car, a black BMW, circles the park. The bearded man, approaching from behind, has one sentence for the town administrator.

"No more mistakes, el Be Merr.

The silencer on the pistol muffles the sound. A single shot is fired at point blank range, striking Beamer in the temple. Instantly, Horst Beamer's head whips and his body stiffens as if dipped in dry ice. The brain function ends, then his body slumps across the seat. The executioner unscrews the silencer tip from the gun. Then the bearded man grabs Beamer's cell phone from his hand and sticks the handgun in Horst's left hand. The man turns slowly and walks to his car. He drives away as if he just got driving directions. The BMW circling the park follows. Both cars drive away leaving the town administrator just before sunrise.

Captain Awad calls the Nigerian Embassy in Washington, DC from a pay phone near a closed ice cream store at the end of Richmond Street in Painesville. The executioner delivers the news.

"The first Fairport Harbor problem has a metal object lodged in his head. He won't be making mistakes or using his cell phone anymore. He has a headache because of the final payment. El Be Merr called us from the bar yesterday. He told us about the other man. We are following that problem. We have traps set if he stops at the right places."

An ambulance was at the scene of a suicide.

"He apparently took his own life. A single shot killed him. A hand gun was recovered at the scene. No other evidence was found, chief," said the Fairport Harbor police corporal. The corporal types his statement at the station and hands it to Chief Otto Mueller. Chief Mueller is disappointed and sad to hear of the tragedy.

Mayor Reese Conway was called soon after the police report was typed.

"Bad news, mayor, our town administrator apparently killed himself this morning. Horst had been drinking heavily last night. The afternoon patrol saw his car at the club yesterday. They said his car was at the club for hours. Early this morning, one of the patrolmen saw his car parked on Plum Street. The car was at Veteran's Park. When they checked the car, Horst was inside. A gun was found in his hand," reports Chief Mueller.

"Pictures of the scene were taken and the car was moved to Mason Renolds' storage garage." The chief continues.

"Otto, this is shocking," says the mayor.

"His neighbor said he saw Beamer's car at Richard Stern's house last night. We are doing an investigation but in all likelihood, he shot himself. Mr. Stern is out of town. A squad went to Stern's house. A young lady said Mr. Stern was out of town on business. She said Horst Beamer did indeed stop at Stern's house last night. She will be stopping to talk with you and me later today." said Police Chief Mueller.

"A young lady was at Mr. Stern's house?" asked the mayor.

"Mayor, this investigation is taking some turns. She is an FBI agent."

A patrol car pulled into the drive as she was about to fall asleep. An officer questioned Agent Monica. She gave a report but withheld the details concerning Horst Beamer's final statement.

When Monica arrived at the mayor's office that afternoon, she is to the point. She pulls out her FBI credentials and explains.

"Mayor Conway, the FBI is working throughout this area. We have a number of agents hunting for remnants of al Qaeda," explains the agent.

"Mayor, we will be looking into this suicide. We would like to search his office at city hall. Did Mr. Beamer have many friends? Is he married?"

"We hired him as a part time administrator two year ago. He wasn't married as far as we know. A number of Mexican visitors and workers were moving into Fairport Harbor so we jumped at the opportunity to have a man in the office that speaks fluent Spanish. His European, German actually, background was an asset because to could talk in many languages. He could also speak, Italian, French, and Arabic. He mentioned on the job application that he was a liaison for a UN relief agency in Lagos, Nigeria fifteen years ago. This man had distant connections. Sometimes he would talk to folks in Washington, DC," said Mayor Conway. Fairport lost a man of many talents."

"That, Mayor Conway, is an understatement."

Later in the day Monica calls Agent Paula Gavalia to update her on the fast moving developments.

"Paula, forget about Horst Beamer. They iced him.

"What? How did it happen?" asked Paula.

"It happened this morning after he woke. As he left Richard's house, he was looking at his cell phone. He walked to his car and drove away. That was the last I saw of him. Police found him with a single gun shot wound to the head. He received a call or message and they set him up for some reason."

"He wasn't planning a suicide. Although that is the preliminary reason for his demise, he didn't kill himself. Keep your guard up; the enemy is close. More checking to do in Fairport Harbor, so I'll be busy the next few days. Horst Beamer's computer, telephone, office, will need to be checked. Cliff knows about the situation. He is working on a car switch. He says nearly every agent is in the field. You won't get any relief for awhile. I'll see you soon," said Agent Monica.

Monica closes by saying, "Tell Mr. Stern that I miss him."

"No way, he is mine when he gets off the booze."

23

Tequila and an Ambulance

Supervisor Moses alters his strategy. He will keep Richard and his agents shifting from place to place while keeping them in public places. The terrorists are somewhat exposed. They will have a difficult time being in public places as their identities are starting to appear on television. The FBI has photos of wanted suspects circulating. Moses calculates that the assassins must lay low or risk being arrested.

He orders Monica and Paula to stay in public places during the day. By choosing museums, libraries, and churches they can feel the security of each place and not be pinned down to one area. This will help his team avoid monotonous duty and keep them moving around. The terrorists that may still be around don't know where Richard has gone since he left town.

Paula and Richard leave the Wickliffe hotel after breakfast. After receiving orders from her boss, she arranges a schedule. A common place to go that is open to the public, is the library. Paula calls around and decides to stop at the closest one, the Willowick Library.

On the way to the library, the conversation begins with a rehash of the sleeping arrangements. Richard was finding little headway in leading Paula to a romantic encounter. She had his number but his persistence would at least earn a B plus.

"You know Paula, the roll-a-way bed isn't that comfortable," complains Richard. Somehow, cupid's arrow might be lining up for him. Luck must be on his side. He is with a beautiful bodyguard. On top of that, he is sleeping at a first class hotel with her. The exception to the romantic rule is, she occupies the king size bed alone.

"The hotel is very relaxing Richard. You can take me here again. Cliff will undoubtedly make a change tonight. He is a boss with a tight hold on Uncle Sam's money. We caught him at the right time. His problem is more than that I'm sure. He has a reason for choosing such a nice place.

"You should refrain from alcohol today. Maybe if you do that, ladies will find you appealing. After all, what type of girl is going to be around a drunk? Try to clean up your style, Richard. This is a promise. You will have a better chance with decent girls if you stay off the booze but I realize you're fighting the terrorists."

"The time to get off the booze is when we finish rounding up this bad element"

The library has a clean, organized décor. They use the internet computers at the library until Supervisor Cliff Moses calls with a new plan.

After Moses reads the report Monica sent him regarding the Fairport Harbor administrator, he orders Paula to stay in Mentor for the night.

Supervisor Moses devises another plan to switch Paula's car. Julie will again work as part of the switch team. Cliff calls for a teleconference so everyone is on the same page. Agents can switch cars with Paula during supper at Perchmans Restaurant.

Perchmans and Harbor Lights are two Grand River restaurants nestled by the river. Because of the parking, Perchmans Restaurant offers an ideal place to make a switch.

Paula and Richard arrive at the restaurant at seven o'clock. They order and Richard decides to have a couple tequila drinks before dinner. Richard was enjoying the atmosphere as the Grand River restaurants are fun places to dine. He was a bit overboard in his conversation with a waitress. He spent time wooing the barmaid as well as the waitress. This upset Paula. Paula had no romantic intentions involving him, but he had a funny style that was likeable. Her job was to protect him. She was concerned with his non-stop drinking. The waitress would have been correct to cut him off but she did the opposite. She kept bringing him fresh drinks. The waitress spoke in a broken accent. She said she was a new waitress. In fact, she was hired because a waitress didn't show up for work that evening. She paid a good deal of attention to Richard. Richard drank a couple margaritas before, during and after his fish dinner. He even made a couple trips to the bar. At one point, he asked the barmaid to use the same brand of tequila. They finish dinner without an argument even though they had differing views about homeland security and civil defense. As they start to leave the restaurant, Paula directs an intoxicated Mr. Stern.

"We are going to leave using the back way," commands Paula

They grab their coats and head out the back door.

"You can be embarrassing. You know you knocked over two drinks and that clumsy act agitated the waitress. You really have a drinking problem," Paula said in a scolding manner.

"No kidding," Richard says sarcastically.

"I'm a connoisseur of liquor."

"The barmaid was making mellow margaritas. There was a problem though. The waitress with the accent served the wrong drink a couple of times. It didn't taste right. I had to dilute it with another drink," he explained.

"What if I ask you to drive? Could you? Can you drive, Richard?"

"Sure can. Where did the car go?" asked Richard.

"Do you think I'm going to let you drive?" Paula asks.

"The staff did a switch of cars while we were inside the restaurant. A couple look-a-like imposters are leaving in our car. We will be driving a Cadillac now. Remember, some of the terrorist escaped. By changing cars, we will throw off anyone watching. We are going to leave out the back door. I really wanted you to drive."

"Paula, you don't have to worry. I can handle any car," says Richard.

"Paula, I knew we could do better on the transportation. I didn't want to say anything. After all, you folks are paying the bills. Where do we end up tonight, Paula your place or mine?" Richard asked jokingly.

He was plenty talkative. That was a sure sign he was feeling high. His drunken manner upset Paula. She decided to test him. She exchanges the ignition key with her personal car key. She really wanted him to drive so she could be the lookout.

"Okay, you drive this time if you're not drunk," she said.

"We are going to slip out of town using Route 283. We'll travel down Lake Shore Boulevard along the lake until we get to Euclid."

"Hey, I'm straight as a judge, I can hold a fair share of liquor," Richard cautiously says. He labors to walk a straight line. His legs aren't as steady as they were two hours before.

Paula flipped Richard the keys to the Cadillac.

"Let's check your reflexes," she says.

Paula used that little check to see if was in control. He caught the keys. She unlocked the doors using the keyless entry button. Inside the car was a GPS system and phone. The car was new, very comfortable and well equipped. Richard became a little big headed as he sat in the cushiony seat. The seat heated as they discussed the exit strategy. As the seat heated, it had a debilitating effect on his disposition. He dropped the keys on the floor as he was trying to find the key slot. He groped along the floor, finally locating them. His vision blurred as he started to dream.

Richard was watching a baseball game from inside a sport's bar in Cleveland. He was with a girl in a booth.

The bartender said this is for your friend. A waitress gave him a wave as if she knew him. He just saw her in Perchman Restaurant. As he finished his beer, the Erie Indian appeared and motioned for him to leave.

Richard's hallucinations were dancing in his head. Another vision appeared.

Something told him to drive to the Beachwood public library. Once there, a school bus pulled up. The driver got out. This man was alone. He is a terrorist. He has a bombers vest with him. This man is going to commit a crime at the library. Richard must stop him.

"Hey, bozo, catch this rock." Richard screamed.

The Erie Indian appeared again. Something flew at the same time. It was an arrow. The arrow struck.

"Hello, hello, Richard, Richard! Are you there? Do you actually think you can drive us?" asked Paula.

"You are drunk." Paula was red-faced mad.

Richard regain his composer but it didn't last.

"I'm a little under the weather. The tequila must be overriding my good judgment. Maybe you better drive Paula. I think I just saw into the future."

Richard could just tell he lit her fuse. His excessive drinking was a bummer. She didn't say anything. She sat silent in the passenger bucket seat.

She thought, "I have to protect this boob. I can straighten him out but am I up for such a challenge?

"Paula, I'm so sorry. I saw something that's going to happen. The Beachwood Library is going to be involved with something. I was going to stop a terrorist there. I yelled to this person, a school bus driver and then my dream ended. I was going to a Cleveland Indians game and I ended up at the library in Beachwood. The Erie Indian appeared in this dream. You try to figure that one out," Richard suggested.

Richard could see she calmed down but he was sinking fast.

"Let's change seats, Richard. You look a little pale. You better explain what comes to you. The bureau needs to know about this vision. Do you really think you saw a terrorist? Was this person a foreigner? How was he dressed?"

Paula grilled Richard as they changed seats. He held onto the car steadying himself as he moved around the car. After sitting down in the passenger seat he thought about the dream.

"I was in a Cleveland sport's bar near the baseball stadium. There's nothing unusual about that Paula, hell, I'm always in a bar."

Richard thought for a second and then it hit him. He recalled something.

"I was with a girl. Who was she? He asks. "Wait a minute, that same waitress was in my dream, she was in the Cleveland sports bar and now she was just in the restaurant, Perchmans Restaurant."

Richard was talking about the waitress in Perchmans Restaurant.

All of a sudden, he was interrupted by the view of Mrs. Rutherford's boat dock. The dock was foggy, and then sparkled as if snow flake were falling in color.

"Mrs. Rutherford, is that you. Is there snow flying," asked Richard?

"Mrs. Rutherford, Mary Ann, stay down, he's got a gun."

Mary Ann gave the terrorists an international hand gesture.

Richard's brain waves seemed to run amuck. He was falling in and out of the real world. The car was spinning like a top. He was looking in a fun house mirror. People are laughing. As he turned to Paula, he was hallucinating. He knew something was wrong with the drink. That wasn't what he ordered.

"Paula, she drugged me."

"She slipped me a Mickey, Paula."

"Grand River, police, this is a 911 emergency. FBI agent is transporting a poisoned victim to Lake East Hospital. We have a medical emergency. I'm heading south on River Street by Rutherford's boat dock. Grand River, do you copy? This is Special Agent PG 109, FBI," said Paula.

"Copy 109, I'm at the stop sign ahead. Continue up the hill, we'll have an ambulance and patrol car ready to assist you. Continue until you see my flashers."

Richard didn't remember what happened. He lost recollection. He was moved to an ambulance and a pretty girl said something about tequila.

Inside Lake Hospital

Inside the recovery room at the hospital were two FBI agents. This was his second FBI interrogation. He didn't have a clue as to what he said.

The two investigators, Agents Ron Roman and Bill Wright took a private jet to save time. They flew to Lost Nation Airport in Willoughby, Ohio. A limo was waiting to take them to Lake East Hospital where they conducted a debriefing with his doctor.

"Doc, we need to know the terrorist plan. At least ask him about the plan. He will tell you a crazy story but record what he says."

Dr. Kay Kuma would not allow the G-men to interview Richard while he was recovering. The G-men asked her if she would conduct a fast interview with him. Reluctantly, she agreed to ask several questions they thought would aid their investigation.

The effects from several substances, a low dose of phenol, psilocybin, and alcohol were almost a deadly combination. One of the chemicals used to spike his drink was a serotonin type drug. The doctor's remedy to detoxify was basic. An intravenous flush was used as they monitored his vitals. The alcohol in his system may have acted to counter the drugs effects. Richard seemed to snap out of it after half a day in recovery. He was somewhat lucky to have knocked over the drinks in the restaurant. The waitress was an assassin. Her deadly mixture didn't get into his system in a sufficient quantity to knock him out.

The doctor related the whole scenario. Dr. Kay told Richard that she asked questions related to the restaurant poisoning. She recorded the conversation as the FBI stood by. The female voice must have started the ball rolling, activating his inner conscience. In the short interview, he related a detailed picture of the enemy.

"Richard, I'm Dr. Kay Kuma. Hypnotizing a victim of foul play sometimes helps them remember. You are recovering from a hallucinogen, a compound tryptamine and alcohol. We also detected phenol in your system. These substances are vacating. We are caring for you. You are relaxing. The questions help to relax the mind. Can you relax? Several questions help you to remember. Tell me what you are thinking. These questions will assemble a puzzle for you. Do you remember your trip to the hospital? Who did this to you? How do they travel? Where can we find them? What is the final target? You will recover, Richard. You will remember, Richard. You are sleepy but tell what you know about their plan. Tell all of this news."

"A spy from Iraq smuggled deadly poisons into Canada. Almost caught in Buffalo, two terrorists are traveling with the chemicals. Parkersburg, West Virginia is another stop. They have encapsulated anthrax spores and a chemical. Members of al Qaeda are meeting at a farm in Springfield, Virginia. This farm is housing a bird population that will be used to spread a nerve agent and anthrax spores around Washington, DC.

"Up ahead are road signs, Route77 and Route 50. The mountains called Shenandoah are along the route. A civil war battle was fought somewhere near Springfield. The farm is near the civil war monument. The farm has pigeons and doves armed with chemicals. That is how it they will bomb Washington, DC.

Doctor Kuma turned to the FBI agents and spoke cautiously.

"He's delusional. You can't possibly trust this story. Give him a couple days and we'll do another interview," she said.

Agent Wright stopped his tape recorder.

"Thanks doc, we have a copy of your interview. You are correct, doc. You have no idea what a delusional man speaks," said Bill Wright.

24

Meetings

Cliff Moses rehearsed his speech inside his car. Cliff played his Indian folk music to effectively calm him down. It was his medicine. After the tunes, he was ready. He would tell fellow agents how the departments were going to nail down the terrorists. Supervisor Cliff Moses of the FBI gives the opening remarks.

Inside a meeting room in Washington, DC were plain clothes agents from four security branches. Supervisor Cliff Moses and his FBI agents were seated next to National Security Agency staff. Secret Service agents were also on hand. U.S. Marshals were just arriving. This special meeting was beginning late at night.

"Terrorist cells emerged over the past months and a major coordinated mission is needed to deliver a sustained volley of body blows to al Qaeda in America."

The brief description of shadowy terrorist leaders that seem to vanish when a capture was imminent was part of the opening dialogue.

Cliff Moses continued, "An FBI campaign was launched eight months prior to round up a band of terrorists that plagued Ohio. Some success was recorded. Later, a Buffalo used car business was busted. Current events, such as the shootout between FBI Agents Roman and Wright, dissected a cell in Parkersburg, West Virginia.

What Supervisor Moses envisioned was an attack on the brains of al Qaeda. FBI leaders believe root problems start in Canada and work their way south into America.

"We are addressing these issues with our friends up north," said Moses.

The FBI would continue to hunt down individual cells and disconnect businesses that feed the criminal virus. A new center of attention would be handled by a joint task force. NSA agents would be taking center stage and calling the shots. The mission is dubbed Operation Virginia Fox. Indications and informer information point to a cell in Virginia. In conjunction with this operation is a

Washington, DC joint stakeout. It is underway by members of the FBI and NSA. That phase of the investigation is the precursor to Operation Virginia Fox.

US Marshalls will team to make arrests as the terrorists are identified. Because a foreign embassy is involved, the State Department is included in this investigation. Homeland Security will have arms around the entire process.

"Gentleman, this operation will be successful. We will deliver body blows to the hierarchy manufacturing and sowing seeds of terror in America. We aim to kill leader numbers one, two, three and however many more or bring them in to face justice. Terrorist leaders have slipped away in the past. Corralling these dirt bags makes this job one of the toughest ever. They are a slippery bunch. Paperwork highlighting the facts of cases will be distributed to all senior staff. We have an informer. This person has been reliable. Your superiors will finish by going over each part of the mission. Final orders will be issued by NSA," says Cliff Moses.

Supervisor Moses finishes and calls his group together to hand out new projected assignments.

"Terrorists are continuing to test our northern border. Canadian authorities are helping us locate nests of al Qaeda. They are trying to stop them. The Canadians face the same problems we do. The religious aspect of the terrorists, conceal some of the elements. In affect, they hide behind the religion. We are going to stop them. The northern border is our operation. NSA is taking the lead role in other areas. With operation Virginia Fox, one of our agents will assist. Agents Wright and Roman, it doesn't look like either of you will be part of the Washington, DC stakeout. Nor will you be involved with the Virginia operation. This news is sure to pain you, Agent Wright. Virginia Fox happens to be a real foxy lady. She is an agent with NSA. We need you and Agent Roman working the northern flank. The FBI is considering sending you two out West for another investigation. Your past work is getting noticed. Don't let it go to your heads. We all work as a team."

Supervisor Moses explains the mission out West.

"A car load of suspected terrorists were picked up crossing into Washington State. They made it to Oregon. It was there that the highway patrol nailed them. This young group is made up of Islamists from a Vancouver, British Columbia mosque. They were coming to America to do special work near Detroit. That is what one of them said during an interrogation. They had wet suits and detonators. You can imagine the work they were going to perform. If called, you will find out what they were planning," commands the supervisor.

"Monica, Julie, and Paula are teaming together on protection assignments. One of them may be needed in Virginia. All these efforts are leaving us a little short on man and woman power. We will get the job done."

Supervisor Moses was commanding in his tone knowing full well his staff could be working long hours.

Days Later

For Richard Stern, this was the second FBI interrogation in which he didn't have a clue as to what he said. Dr. Kuma, used hypnosis to worm into his subconscious. The FBI agents simply taped what was said. After the second interview Richard didn't have anything new to add. He recovered from the effects of the drugs so the doctor released him to the FBI and recommended out-patient after care for the alcohol problem.

Stern, still under protection, was picked up by Agent Gavalia. Paula convinced Supervisor Moses to let the lady agents work with Stern on his memory. Moses reluctantly agreed.

"What did I say, Paula?" Richard asked as they strolled into the Mayfield Village library.

"You have a bad memory. Do you remember kissing me?"

"Now that would be indelible. No way would that be forgotten if you presented such a reward. Just the thought makes my heart flutter. Tell me you're not kidding," pleads Mr. Stern.

"If you stay sober, good things happen and you will remember," she explains

Paula kept firing a steady stream of reasons to break the alcoholic temptation. Her female sensuality had a positive effect on Richard. Monica joined in later as she watched Paula carefully table his drinking habit. The shift rotated and Julie became part of the bodyguard service. Paula relieved Julie. The team of FBI agents and a counselor worked to restore Richard's sanity. Moses wanted his team back on regular assignments. He wanted to know more about the terrorist plans out West. The more his agents learn about future terrorist plans the better. Moses knew Richard well enough. Moses saw plenty of failed attempts at recovery, even his own.

"He'll be back on the bottle. If we can find out a little more, we will be saving lives. Stern will have to fall a few more times. Mark my words, Julie and be prepared to copy down anything Stern says. Paula is trying to rehabilitate the drunk. I take my hat off to her for that." He says to Agent Julie.

25

Role Change

Agents Roman and Wright studied their notes. They had a map spread out across the table. On the map blocks were notated with the dates of terrorist encounters. Agent Wright commented and had a theory to share.

"Every time we investigate a terrorist cell it seems to migrate to another area."

Bill Wright used text blocks to enclose details for his sidekick. He theorized about the al Qaeda terrorists and the mosques he believed held the radicals.

"Ron, my theory is evolving into a national theme. They have maybe five leaders in America. These guys are ruthless murderers."

"Multiple operations are going on across the country. The al Qaeda organization is being run from a head of state. Somewhere on this side of the globe the main killers hide. A cell leader reaches North America. The cell recruits, multiples, and spreads out into regions. They shift cell members among three working groups. If one group is under attack, the members escape to another region where they keep from losing most of their forces. It is a cancer. We have to kill all of the diseased cells," says Wright

Roman understands the complex nature of the problem. He adds more.

"It is a world disorder. Many nations are fighting the same disease. The Pope even mentioned this problem. Radical Muslims are destroying their own religion."

Agent Roman's opinion has religious implications as he refers to the Roman Catholic Pope.

"Bill, I agree with that theory. A personal view is this. We are fighting a religious war, started many centuries ago. Now listen, what can we do to stop this? Well, Cliff called and said the next assignment is for real. Get your fishing pole ready, pal. We are going to Washington."

"Washington, DC with Paula, I'm for going there," says the Casanova type agent.

"No, not Washington, DC, this time we go out West. Paula will handle the DC job. We are needed where the big ones roam. Washington State and Oregon, their rivers are loaded with chinook, steelhead, and sockeye salmon. We are two of the best FBI agents in the country. Maybe the bureau is giving us a reward for the job in Parkersburg."

Bill and Ron give each other high fives. Cliff Moses told them they could be away from Cleveland for a month.

Springfield, Virginia

An FBI search of public records raised suspicion. One farm in Springfield, Virginia netted interesting information on the owner. That farm in particular would be checked out as a priority. The farm owned by Klalil Mahdi is the one that fits Richard Stern's description. Agents kept close surveillance on Mr. Mahdi's visitors. He frequently had lady friends visit, but never on the weekends.

FBI and NSA officials were called together. Senior officers meet in a closed door meeting with the Homeland Security Director to begin operation Virginia Fox. The plan is to gather inside evidence on Klalil Mahdi and decide if this is the suspected terrorist staging area. The hypnotic information Richard Stern supplied was not enough to turn a farm inside out. Indeed, this is a farm in Springfield, Virginia, where the suspected operation could be headquartered. The director would need more information.

"Is Klalil Mahdi operating a farm to deliver a terrorist attack? Were chemicals unrelated to farming stored at the farm?" asked the director.

NSA asked and received permission from a federal judge to install a bug. Agent Tex Williams would install a patch into the phone system near the property. He would be assisted by Lady Jane. Jane would be the front door person who would make initial contact with the subject. She would soften Mr. Mahdi's behavior. NSA leadership recognized Jane's capabilities. She had undercover experience and Miss America style which fit the mission well. The operation would take time. A timeline was devised to leverage several contacts with Mr. Mahdi. Because of her demeanor, Lady Jane could easily get close to Klalil Mahdi, after a trust was built.

A background check of Klalil Mahdi revealed arrests were made for child endangerment, trafficking in pornography and prostitution. He paid fines and received probation each time. It appeared Mr. Mahdi had a passion for the opposite sex. That would create a natural weakness NSA could exploit.

"Agent Jane, your womanly talent is needed again. Who is Mr. Mahdi's boss? We need to find out what chemicals are on the property. He may have anthrax hidden on the farm for all we know. You need to get into his head and learn about the operation. Use extreme caution."

The first steps in your mission will be very dangerous. If he is up to his eyeballs in terrorist activity, he will be super cautious. Learn what you can. We want to send in Tex Williams and let him search the property. He will make a nighttime visit. Don't take any chances. You work for the gas company. We will have the IntraGas Company make contact and arrange for you to sample the air in Mahdi's basement."

We believe Mr. Mahdi will harm you if you are discovered. We hope you will accept this challenging role but you can back out right now. We will understand."

"Gentlemen, I'll get Tex in there. Just give this agent a little time. After a while, Mr. Mahdi will be yours. I have the tools and the potion," claimed the beautiful agent.

Agent Jane requested a partner and the NSA staff felt a joint operation would aid the spirit of homeland security. Cliff Moses would pick two candidates. His choices were easy, although he wanted Agent Monica to be the partner.

This partner would need to be a person equal to Jane in appearance. Both Monica and Paula had the right stuff. NSA decided to take Paula only because she was a little younger than Monica and the leadership felt Paula would be more attractive. Any advantage would be a plus and her attractions were more pronounced which offered Mr. Mahdi a greater temptation.

26

Libraries and Change

Paula continued with the same strategy, staying in public places. She was cautious about being in a closed setting where someone could corner them. They continued visiting busy places, such as libraries, museums, antique shows. She selected travel routes where traffic was heavy. Busy streets in suburbs outside of Cleveland were the running lanes. This movement would keep potential assassins from planning a hit.

Richard Stern sat in the Mayfield Library reading the newspaper headlines about the West Virginia shootout. Paula was blissfully reading the Woman's Weekend Journal. The Lake County Voice, a local newspaper, went into detail about the shootout with government agents. The paper mentioned the ability of two FBI agents to follow the terrorist's tracks. The newspaper article was sub titled, TERRORISM BY CAR. The article said terrorists were busy shuttling cars from Detroit and Buffalo through Cleveland and Ashtabula to sites further south. The reason for trafficking in cars was to hide terrorist movements. Used cars were effective because cars could be dismantled or abandoned. The terrorists communicated through legitimate businesses. They opened convenience stores to exchange money. Legitimate looking convenience stores would act as staging areas. In a sense it was a terrorist depot. Terrorists with little command of English could easily stay overnight in a store until moved to a safe house. The safe house was often called the nest.

The newspaper article continued, elaborating on the religious aspects of terrorism.

The terrorist organization operated inside a network of religious institutions. Terrorists relied on the commonality of their religion. Being too far from a mosque was the weak link. A small army of radical fanatics operated freely inside the religious institutions. According to terrorist experts, terrorist cells are moving south. In North America, mosques in Canada are stretched far from terrorist businesses, which can expose a weakness.

Mr. Big, a kingpin in the radical element, established one huge nest in Fairport Harbor, Ohio. That nest was a construction site with a large circus tent erected near the river. His base extended from Grand River across Lake Erie. Washington, DC was the major source of money and command. Recruits were drawn from Toronto, Detroit, and Buffalo. His operation was destroyed when FBI agents and Lake County sheriffs converged after tips exposed the pending terrorist attack.

Mr. Big used his attorneys and shadows to hide when the operation imploded. He seemed to vanish along with his lieutenants.

The newspaper asks questions. How many cells are in America? How does al Qaeda get into this country? Where are the leaders? Is congress ever going to fix the border security problem? The journalist speculates that an informer is a cell member.

"No he isn't, he's a drunk," comments Richard, the recovering alcoholic.

Indeed, Richard is beginning to understand his problem with alcohol. Paula is the lecturer, guiding Richard. Father Pete used his spiritual words to point the alcoholic in the right direction. Paula is masterful in her encouragement. She uses the power of female persuasion. Richard welcomed Paula's guidance. His honesty was suspect. Surely, his lustful hope is a driving force. What is really helpful is the fact that Richard found a friend who cares for him. While she is much younger, a bond began to develop between the two. For Paula, this is a humanitarian project.

On Sunday, she took him to church at Saint John's Cathedral in Cleveland. That afternoon, a new bell did toll. Paula's humanitarian project would change direction. Monica would take over and move in a radically different direction.

Supervisor Cliff Moses couldn't help but detect close personal involvement transpiring between Paula and Richard. He did not want his agents forming any personal relationship with protected citizens. Luckily, the supervisor didn't have to intervene. Moses was delivered a timely solution. NSA chose Paula as the partner. NSA preferred to use Paula rather then Agent Monica as part of the team to launch operation Virginia Fox. This change was a boon, for it aided Cliff's management. Cliff Moses readily agreed to the change but he knew Monica would feel she was slighted.

Sunday night Supervisor Moses called Monica and asked her to come to the office. Monica thought this must be big, a call from the boss Sunday night. She hurried over to FBI headquarters. It was big news all right, big and bad.

"NSA had a short list of FBI agents for project Virginia Fox. Your name was first on the list. Monica, you were the one and then a change was made. NSA decided at the last minute to use someone similar in appearance to NSA Agent Lady Jane. You didn't meet the criterion so you will switch with Paula. She will work with the NSA agent. You will relieve her for the next week."

"Cliff, this is not right. You know this is not right, Cliff," she cries.

"All staff leaders thought you would be picked. Please understand it was a decision that was made beyond this department's control. Personally speaking, you are more qualified, but NSA wants Paula and they have the final say. Tomorrow morning you will relieve Agent Gavalia," lamented Supervisor Moses.

Monica left Cliff's office deeply dejected. Her hope was to be one of the leaders in operation Virginia Fox. A mission of that magnitude would be a ticket to supervisory status. She was stunned.

Paula's relief arrived on Monday. Unfortunately for Monica, she was the one doing the relieving. Monica would be the bodyguard for the next week as Paula was assigned to operation Virginia Fox. Monica had high hope for an out of state mission where she could showcase her crime fighting ability. That idea was dashed.

"Monica, Cliff called me last night. You have every right to be upset. Please don't be bummed with the change that was made. You will get a fresh assignment. We have worked together for over two years now. Something like this was bound to happen," says a sorrowful Agent Paula.

"Working with Richard is tough at times. He is off the booze now and he is becoming a pretty handsome guy. Take care of him and stay alert. I told Richard if he stayed sober decent ladies would find him. You will see a changed man. He is much better now. See you soon."

Paula left the hotel room knowing full well her partner was disappointed. Saying anything more was sure to fan a fire.

Richard entered the room as Paula departed. He was fresh after a morning shower.

"Changing of the guard, I see," comments Richard.

Monica was not happy at all. Richard could sense a woman brooding over something.

"Yes, it is a turn that came too soon. Sorry, Mr. Stern, things didn't go the right way. You are not privy to the details but someone is bummed out in this room. Let's get out of here before anything more goes foul," she says.

Richard and Monica leave the hotel.

"How about a nice dinner after a walk in the mall, Monica, the FBI is buying?"

"No thanks, food doesn't interest me right now."

The Beachwood Hotel wasn't far from the mall. Monica and Richard walked in the mall for two hours. Richard was determined to lift Monica's spirits. His aimless chat wasn't working. Unable to inspire the unhappy agent, Richard resorted to one of his favorite broken heart remedies.

"Monica, let's go to a baseball game. My old girl friends used to enjoy games at the ballpark. We aren't that far away."

They drove into Cleveland only to find out the game was away.

"See that's the story of my life. Poor Monica is shutout again," she moans.

"We can watch it on TV. There are plenty of places around here to watch an afternoon game. Monica, baseball is a sure way to get rid of the blues. You don't have to be blue. Look, over there, there's a sports bar. They will have the game on TV. We can have an afternoon dinner and watch the game when it comes on."

Monica wasn't a drinker. Her chance to deal the cards was a way to even the score. Slighted as she was, she could turn the table on Paula's coup.

The game being played was a business man's special, an afternoon game played in Minnesota. The sports bar was half-filled with business patrons. Monica's mood seemed to improve as she was among well dressed business folks, and the place was very upscale. She could relax without much worry.

Richard timed the idea right, as Paula would never go for the sport's bar scene. Richard's disease was patiently waiting for this blunder. He waltzed up to the bar and had a quick shot of blackberry brandy. That drink was like starting a fire with gasoline. His streak of abstinence was broken. He ordered two twenty-two ounce mugs of beer, thinking to himself, "If Monica doesn't want a beer, both of these are mine."

He quickly downed three gulps on his way back to the table. It was a walk back to his past. He was on his way to drunkenness.

"Monica, you can have one of these. Nobody is going to see you in this booth. Besides, it is dark in here."

Monica paused for a moment. The rejection she felt was overwhelming. Jealousy ran a track across her common sense. It was much like a flaw on a record. The song plays over the hiccup and repeats. A mission lost to her partner was planted in her mind.

Though it wasn't Paula's fault, Monica placed some blame on her. She could get back at her partner if Mr. Stern started drinking again. She lost self-control. Right and wrong were pushed aside. She gave in. She drank a beer as the two waited for the game to start. Monica was only going to have one, but Richard was a doctor with medicine. Richard drank two more and bought another for Monica when she went to the restroom.

He visited the restroom and while there the bartender mentioned something about a new drink for ladies. He said it could help overcome a woman anxiety about sex. Richard didn't care for the implications, but the bartender winked at him later.

The alcoholic was back to his old form, picking up right where he was when he stopped drinking. Though his break from alcohol use was short, the return was like riding a bike. He was back on the sauce. He would never have just one. The cycle of alcohol use was like a bowling machine. Richard pushed reset and a new rack was ready to be downed. The place was clean, comfortable, and had medicine.

They ordered chicken wings and cheese sticks. Monica drank another beer. She was becoming drunk, which loosened her tongue. Richard was all ears, consoling in a careful manner. Her lost assignment was demeaning.

"Don't tell me that I'm not worthy, attractive, and a good agent," says Monica, holding back her tears. She grabs the glass and polishes off the drink.

Richard sympathizes with her, choosing words to mask a walk in Adam and Eve's garden. Richard quickly orders two more beers, lengthening the rope of a spiraling mood.

The game ended in two and half hours. Enough time to put a buzz on the brain. Monica and Richard drove back to the hotel and went straight to the bar. A fun time would continue as happy hour was near. Soon reality was forgotten.

They requested a bar room controller to play a trivia game. More drinks and intellectual challenge pushed the evening clock along. It was ten thirty and enough alcohol was consumed by both game players. Temptation is not easily warded off.

"Monica, you have brought me back to life. You saved my life in New York. Let's get out of here so we don't get in trouble," kindly said by a Lucifer.

Monica was very drunk at this stage. Richard was masterful in timing a ceremonial toast to good life and liberty.

"We'll have one for the walk to the room," said Richard.

"You'll be the bride and I'll be the groom," he added.

Monica went along with the charade as they took the elevator back to the hotel room. Her professional manner was spoiled but ragged disappointment was partially replaced by the cumulative affects of the day.

Richard requested a bottle of Chardonnay to finish out the evening. The bartender obliged believing the couple was a consenting pair.

"The bellhop will deliver, sir."

"Room 310 and don't be surprised if Mr. and Mrs. Stern are busy." Mr. Stern devilishly echoed in a voice audible enough for others to hear.

The two melancholy characters, neither playing with a full deck of reality, worked their way toward the elevator. Monica paused to kiss Mr. Stern for a day of relaxation. Her temptress touch was fire brand with emotion. Gaining lift from the embraces, passion ruled as seconds ticked. The feeling of bodily contact created the next stepping stone to points well known.

Monica had her shoes in her hand as they arrived on floor three. Richard asked if he could carry the bride over the threshold. His lame effort wasn't to be, but the effect of the booze was funny for both.

"Sorry, Monica, the ship must be pulling out of the port. The boat is rocking." He tastefully admitted his weakness and drunken state.

They found the room and kissed again at the door. Monica had shut her eyes to a man twenty years older. She could feel the suppleness and her own desire working toward a reward. They unlock each other and the door.

The move to the bed was not without a mistake. Looking back, the door was nearly open. There was a tap on the door as the bellhop arrived with the wine. The bellhop wheeled in a cart and iced decanter. He flipped two long stem glasses right side up. Richard and Monica toyed with each other. Monica had her jacket off and exposed a handgun that caused the bellhop to drop his jaw. She removed the holster as Richard peeled a five dollar bill for the wine delivery.

The young bellhop received a glimpse of a beautiful woman unfastening her shirt and pants as Richard motioned for him to leave. The bellhop was mesmerized not just by the pistol on the nightstand but also by a woman in a provocative state. The live show moved along for him until Richard stuck the five in his hand and moved him out the door. Richard fastened the chain lock on the door and moved to the bed.

Monica slid under the covers as Richard worked off his shoes and shirt. His pants were next as he moved to join Monica. The heat of each embrace was compassionate without thought. The kiss lasted as he pulled on the waistband of his underwear. The timely kisses had progressed, intensified, and enhanced his aging body. Monica on the other hand responded fondly as she was radiant, clean, and balanced. Her womanhood, obviously well cared for, worked to strengthen Richard. Since both partners were drunk, and new to each other, foreplay was limited and slightly awkward as Richard lost control. Monica lustfully played with the person she should be protecting. The union did not last long. The alcohol stained good reason. Monica's conscience had reservations. An opposite feeling of happiness was at work. She felt emotionally imprisoned with the union, but the moment of passion overruled the oath of good reason.

For Richard, satisfaction, a male mystic, weighed heavy on the moment. He knew pleasure was not a fair trade. He held her down as if Samson was reincarnated. Samson, he was not. Monica flipped him off as she regained a measure of sanity.

She dashed for the bathroom with a blanket in tow. She was fully aware of the break in Cliff Moses' rule. The ordeal was frightening for Monica. A career could be ruined by a lesser mistake. She sat on the floor, her back against the bathroom door, crying. A small pool of fluid was near the inside of her legs. Her ordeal was even worse as she thought about the consequences of the night. She wiped herself clean still sobbing.

The sob stopped when Richard tapped on the door.

"Monica, someone is at the door." She grabbed her robe off the hook. Almost flying in the air, she drew the robe lash together. In an instant, she was at the nightstand, reaching for the pistol.

Monica motioned for Richard to move to the side of the door. She grabbed a pen from the nightstand and quickly wrote a note.

"Tap, tap, Police officer, is anyone in there?"

The person outside the door kept asking.

Monica slid the note to Richard. It said, "Richard, tell him to have the manager call this number, 310 now."

Monica raises her gun, motioning to Richard to tell the person outside their door to call the room by phone.

"Tap, police, is anyone in there."

"You have to call the room by phone. We don't open the door for strangers, not even the police," says Richard.

"We will get the manager, sir. We will have the manager call you."

Monica grabbed her pants and shirt. Going braless, she dropped the robe and put on a sweater over her shirt. Next she put on her black slip on shoes. She stuffed the holster into the robe. Richard found his underwear under the bedspread and grabbed his pants. He was hopping around like a chicken trying to put his pants on. He ended down on the floor to put them on. He found his shoes, slipped them on along with a pull over tee shirt.

Both of them were still intoxicated but sobering fast.

"Open the door when I tell you."

She pointed the gun at the door and said,

"Now, Richard, open the door."

Monica used a mirror with a handle on it to scan the corridor. Nobody was in the hall. They looked together. Outside the room the hall was empty.

"Time to go, move to the stairwell. Grab the jackets," she ordered.

The jackets were near the door on a chair. Richard snatched them on the fly

The phone started to ring as they ran down the hall. They used the back stairwell and made it to the back exit. Inside the hall they donned coats. They exited the back of the hotel. The car was parked on the side of the building. A police car was parked next to their car. Monica wasn't sure what was going to happen. She was tired. She needed fresh air to clear out the cob webs from her mind.

"Keep walking, don't look back, I don't know who or what is going down; just keep moving away from the hotel," said Monica.

They walked for about two miles and hailed a taxi. The Indian driver only came to the country five months ago.

"America is fun and exciting, wouldn't you agree?" asked the taxi driver.

They drove to a run down motel where they checked in for the night. Richard was relegated to the floor.

Monica was very ashamed. She prayed to God that night that her weakness wouldn't lead to greater problems.

Richard's dream started and ended fast as he went to sleep.

The police officer was checking the damage on the front of a rental car.

"According to the computer, the people registered to that car are in 310, officer. They paid for this room for six days. Says here they are staying until Wednesday. They came in last Thursday. Says here a Mr. and Mrs. Paula Gavalia are driving that car. Mr. Gavalia was with another woman last night, officer. Don't ask, sir! Can't tell you anything more. We are like Las Vegas. You never know who stays in this hotel," said the manager.

Richard woke up first and went to the bathroom. He took a shower and came out to find Monica talking on the cell phone.

"OK, thank you so much, Mr. Crammer. You have been a great help and such a relief. We were very concerned about trouble," said Monica.

"Mr. Stern, someone hit our car last night while it was parked at the hotel. The police were at the hotel trying to notify the owner last night."

"The boss wanted to know what happened. Cliff stopped at the hotel early this morning. The manager let him in the room. I told him everything that happened last night." Monica moaned, fearing for her job.

"We are not staying there ever again. We'll go back and get our clothes. Forget last night ever happened. Don't ever bring this up to anyone. You promise, Mr. Stern? You promise?"

"Monica, please forgive me. You were so attractive. It is a promise. Never, never, Monica, I promise. Monica, my attraction for you is real." Richard Stern pleaded.

"Give me a break, Mr. Stern. You are a drunk and you took advantage of the situation," She yelled.

"Tomorrow is the last day. Julie takes over, thank God. Cliff said a change is needed. He was concerned about the situation but thought professionalism would rule. He said he should have seen the problem when Paula got the assignment. Cliff said he doesn't need to know anything more. The matter is closed. Cliff Moses is a great leader," said a relieved Agent Monica.

Richard Stern didn't tell Monica about the dream. He wanted her to like him but he knew his drinking caused the whole mess. He began to feel sorry for himself.

27

Washington, DC

The Nigerian Embassy itself was a victim of phony schemes. Oil money was skimmed from the Nigerian government by unscrupulous terrorists disguised as Islamic charity organizers. The Mahdi brothers were always in line for a hand out. Some of the charity money funded the Mahdi bird operation.

Klalil Mahdi devised a food that could woo birds to land in certain areas. The Mahdi bird food is a formula he invented at his Buffalo safe house. Five years of experiments with sea gulls along Lake Erie gave him the impetus to expand. He convinced a Detroit banking group into loaning him funds. His terrorist cell expanded when he bought two more safe houses, a store, and a farm. The Buffalo operation was sold to Mr. Big's lieutenants. Mr. Big's men worked with special gases and caged birds. The safe house was used as a practice lab by terrorist interns, who occasionally worked at another terrorist operation across the street. That business, a used car dealership, was busted. Most of the real lab was moved to Toledo, Ohio, before a fire destroyed the safe house. In Toledo, Mr. Mahdi continued the bird research. Here he found sympathizers with pharmaceutical knowledge. He made one more move after he learned of an Iraqi spy, who had special chemicals.

Mahdi's devious ways convinced him to plan a Washington, DC operation. The farm near DC became an experimental lab. The operation grew to become a pilot plant. Mr. Mahdi's bird food served two purposes. When spread in an area, it marks a drop zone and the birds land. The birds are loaded at the farm to carry poison. When they land, the wind spreads contamination airlifted by the birds.

Captain Awad and Klalil Mahdi converged in separate cars near the Washington Monument. Mr. Mahdi championed the "Mahdi Easter surprise." He casually talks terrorism with Captain Awad on 15th Street.

"Captain Awad, today this is a drop zone. The birds know this area by the food that is here for them."

Klalil Mahdi opens a package and spreads the formula. He sprinkles bottled water on the food. Soon a flock of pigeons are at their feet feeding in a frenzy. It was like chumming the water with blood soaked meat. The trick is to have the right birds land. Mahdi's birds know the scent is activated by the water.

"You will see another example when I conduct an experiment at the embassy. Then you will say, Mr. Klalil Mahdi, you have the perfect weapon."

"The infidels will fall ill on a mass scale," says Mahdi as he smiles as if talking to the devil.

"Mr. Mahdi, I will have several soldiers ready to sacrifice. They will dispense the food and water. We must make sure this plan works. Your birds must carry the chemicals to each selected area. If the pigeons follow as you have outlined, America will be taught a great lesson. The U. S. Capitol is the first target. Then Russell, Dirksen, and the Hart office buildings are next. We will need a wind from the southwest."

"The men will be instructed to water down the nests of food if the rains don't come. April showers bring the gas attack, but you need your birds to deliver the chemicals. The government has biological and chemical detectors installed around Washington. This plan will hit them before they can respond," says the captain.

"My trained birds, two hundred of them so far, will cause mass casualties. Captain Awad, Easter Sunday, do you agree? Mr. Mahdi asks.

"Yes, this is the day. America will have gas, gas pains. America will come down with a bad case of Toban and Sarin gas, ha, ha, ha," laughs Mr. Mahdi.

28

Infiltrate

The Mahdi farm was situated in semi-rural country. A town near the farm, Indian Springs, was thirty miles from Washington, DC. The town has a decent school, stores, and a distribution depot for natural gas. A major road, Interstate 395, was close to the town.

The road to the farm was asphalt covered, pock marked by indented holes from winter plows. Many old farms in the area were converted into housing developments. The aged gas lines that served the farms were still in operation. Natural gas wells dug on farm property long ago still feed the main artery of the IntraGas Company system.

The Mahdi chicken farm was not unusual. However, Mr. Mahdi had exotic birds penned inside one barn and he trained these birds. Pigeons and doves found sanctuary in another barn next to the house. The red pigeon barn had holes in the roof. The birds would fly daily coming and going willy-nilly. The birds flyway passed by Reagan International Airport.

Birds were used as messengers to troops in the field during wars. Mr. Mahdi considered a new use for his birds. Mahdi trained the pigeons to fly to College Park near the University of Maryland. Once there, an associate would radio Mahdi with news of a landing. Mahdi timed the birds and worked on a schedule the birds would follow. Mahdi successfully trained the birds to land in new areas.

Klalil Mahdi's work with the birds could be used to export terrorism. He refined his diabolical plan. The birds would be used for a deadly drop. Mahdi worked many experiments with the pigeons and doves. Recording the bird's payload carrying capabilities, the distances they could travel with varying weights. Satisfied that his experiments could pass muster, he offered his plan to Captain Awad, since his help and approval was needed to hatch a far larger bird attack.

NSA and the FBI were cooperating better. Instead of two independent agencies, there was reciprocation between them. Both departments could share computer notes and agents would team on special cases.

The team of Tex Williams, and Agents Jane and Paula brainstormed with Assistant Director Jake Jefferies to build a solid plan. Project Virginia Fox started out with plans to exercise dogs near the farm. That idea was tabled because the group thought animals were sometimes unpredictable. They argued pros and cons of an infiltration route. Concerned, lacking good ideas, they decided to distract Mahdi outside the farm through a staged auto accident. That idea was shelved for a more daring plan. The team decided to advance Agent Jane right to the front door of Mahdi Farm. She would face Mahdi straight up. Agreed was a simple lady in your face plan. A meter reader visit would suffice.

The FBI had a Mahdi in prison when they broke the terrorist ring in Fairport Harbor. The FBI had captured Abdul Mahdi, thought to be a brother, as he tried to break from his Fairport Harbor convenience store. Convicted for dealing in arms, dangerous chemicals, explosives and aiding terrorists, an Ohio judge put him away. He wasn't any help identifying senior accomplices. The FBI gave up trying to pry information from him. The tight lipped Abdul Mahdi was sent back to prison in Lucasville, Ohio.

Agent Jane carried a tiny camera for the first visit. She kept the device from view using a belt buckle on her jeans. Pretending to be a utility intern, working for IntraGas, Paula and Jane stopped at the Mahdi Farm. She poured on the charm when Mr. Mahdi came to the door in person. She was surprised, expecting a guard to intercept her.

Agent Jane had a company van to drive. Her IntraGas coveralls were baggy, hiding most of her female detail. When she took off her hat, the flowing blond hair caused a sunshine smile to break from Mr. Mahdi.

Agent Jane made no excuse about her love for farmers and their lifestyle.

"Mr. Mahdi, we are gas company meter readers. IntraGas Company is sending us to every customer's house in the area to inspect gas lines. We don't do repairs. If we detect a problem, we report it. Today, we check this side of the road. Monday we will be on the other side of the street. Grandma and Grandpa had a farm. Not as big as this one, you see. You must be a rich man. Sorry, sir, I got carried away by the farm. It's just that farms are so cool," said Lady Jane.

"The regular woman that is normally working with us is sick so we are on our own. We are just temporary employees but we know what we are going. She is a good teacher, Mrs. Hampton that is. The utility company sent us to get a reading on the gas meter. Everyone in this area is on our list. Some gas meters have malfunctioned; don't read correctly and even leaked gas. That rarely happens though. Like I said, Paula and I have to check every home, business and farm in this area that has a gas hookup. The company's been training us for six weeks. I have a business card, see."

She unfastens the latch on her coveralls to reveal a well developed woman. Mr. Mahdi is somewhat consumed by the attraction.

"Well, young lady, time is not on my side, there's no gas problem here," says Mr. Mahdi.

"They really want us to check, Mr. Mahdi. We both got jobs straight out of high school. We are both going to college in the evening. Mom can't afford to pay tuition. Will you let us check your meter Mr. Mahdi? We get four bucks each. This won't take long, sir. The detector is real fast. It can even detect a small leak."

Agent Jane wasn't sure if she made a successful pitch. She sensed Mahdi was edgy. She added more show.

"You don't have to worry about my muddy shoes. The lady of the house won't know we were here. We won't dirty anything. The coveralls and shoes can stay on the porch."

Jane struggled with her shoes and continued the act.

"Mrs. Mahdi doesn't have to worry, sir. We clean up any mess. The gas company is paying us by the job, kind of like piece rate, so we have to hustle."

"Well alright, move along then. I'll show you to the gas meter. Nobody ever goes to that side of the cellar."

Mr. Mahdi fell for the act. He was awash in misaligned thoughts as Agent Jane worked to remove her coveralls.

"It happened last time, Mr. Mahdi. The elbow gets caught in my coveralls. Can you help?" asks Jane.

Her perfume nestled in Mr. Mahdi's nostrils as they worked to free her arm. A slight cleavage was presented as Agent Jane did her best to remove the coverall.

"Paula, please come help us," yelled Jane.

The unprofessional manner the two ladies portrayed helped Mr. Mahdi reach a conclusion that the girls are young and dumb.

His thought was naughty as he worked to free Agent Jane.

He thought to himself. "These two girls have much to learn about business."

Paula is gyrating in the van; music from the radio is distracting her. The first stage of the act is working well. The youthful workers are care free, on a mission with no supervision. She acts as if she misses what is going on.

"As I said earlier, Mr. Mahdi, IntraGas thinks gas leaks are coming from old meters. All of these tiny leaks are collectively costing them big bucks. Oh, that's what they say. If it were really bad, you would have smelled it. Gas can roam about so I want to be very thorough in my check of the lines. Your farm is so wonderful. I dream to some day have a farm of my own. Men who farm can be so exciting," says the meter reader.

Mr. Mahdi's attitude shifted gears. He didn't have anything in the house that was going to cause him a problem.

"Yes, young lady, by all means, let me show you the way. This monitor you have, will it tell us whether we are getting close to the leak?"

"We'll see the screen turn color as we approach the danger, Mr. Mahdi." said Jane.

As they move close to the meter, the detector goes dead.

"Oh no, Mr. Mahdi, the unit went dead. I forgot to charge the unit. You were almost the last customer to check. I'm so sorry, Mr. Mahdi. We can't come back today. Is Monday OK?

"No, it is not," says Mr. Mahdi.

"Mr. Mahdi, I'm so sorry. We can come back tomorrow. I'll charge this up today. Mr. Mahdi, please let me finish tomorrow. The company won't accept the data if the charge was low. If they find out, we are in trouble. Please don't tell. I can help you on the farm. Do you need help, Mr. Mahdi," she asks?

"I will be here alone tomorrow. Yes, you finish tomorrow. I'm short-handed on the weekend. Now that you asked, you could earn forty buck tomorrow. The work is tough. Be here at eight in the morning," says Mr. Mahdi.

"Sir, I can handle it. You say what to do. Farmers are the greatest people."

Mr. Mahdi follows Jane up the steps and watches as they leave. Jane and Paula wave good bye.

Agent Jane hops in the van and describes the experience. She finishes with a touch of girl talk.

"Paula, Mahdi likes farm girls."

29

Going East Monica

Cliff Moses paid a visit to Mr. Stern after hearing from Monica. He was in no mood for idle chat. Moses could light a fire with words but in his drive to the flea bag motel, he calmed down. He played a CD to gain control of his emotion. The Indian background music released the tension inside Cliff Moses. He seemed to have the right balance of authority for every occasion. This day was no different. He quickly reassured Monica that she would have another chance.

"Monica, take the car back to headquarters. A case in Grand River Village will have you busy. Case GRV 03 is on your desk for review. A body was found floating in Grand River. This could be the waitress that never showed up for work the day Mr. Stern was poisoned. You clear your head then follow up with a visit to the Grand River police station. Find out how this might tie to Stern's poisoning. Take a look at the case and take the rest of the day off," ordered the supervisor.

Moses adds final direction.

"We have a back log of cases and it isn't slowing down. Put your detective brain to work and solve these mysteries. Also, you can plan on being out of the Cleveland area. Pack clothes for a stay near DC and Virginia. A gut feeling is, you will be with Paula."

"Have Julie return to the hotel with you to pick up your belongings. Mr. Stern and I need some time to discuss his future."

"Yes sir, boss," says Agent Monica.

Cliff tossed the car keys to Monica. She didn't stick around. Cliff Moses sounded a bit like her Father in that he didn't dwell on the poor judgment. She was also relieved that he didn't ask any questions about the previous day. Mostly, she was relieved that he didn't fire her.

"Stern, you can really stretch your luck. When driving here, a message from heaven appeared. Fortunately for you, God sent this message. He whispered in my right ear. Let Stern choose any or all of these. Stern finds rope, arrows, and a bottle of whiskey. He can tie up more terrorists or hang himself. He can fight the enemy or stick an arrow in our back. He can down the booze and let the future wash away. God is your lifeline, Stern. Stop picking up the booze. Paula said you were doing better. Sure we can use your tips, but we can also carry on without them. We spent a bundle protecting you. The money was well spent when you supplied decent information, but not at the expense of my people. I might ship you out with Agent Roman and Wright."

"People in this department spend years cultivating a career. Mistakes are made and people get hurt. You embark on an indiscretion to unhinge a decent agent, especially an agent that is protecting you. We are a family, Stern. You took advantage of a family member. That doesn't sit very well."

"This is what is going to happen. Tomorrow you are on your own until I get a handle on other matters. Today, Julie will help you until midnight. Then she is going to call and say the prince of buffoons has been released to his own recognizance. Protecting you from you and the terrorists requires agents we don't have. Are you willing to drink yourself into a grave? Get some help, Stern, join AA."

"You find a place to stay, but don't go back home. I don't have agents to keep a watch on someone that takes advantage of our people. The fact is I have everyone in the field right now so shipping you out isn't such a bad idea."

Moses thought about what he said. Shipping Stern to the West Coast might not be such a bad idea.

"I'm really sorry, Mr. Moses. Maybe I will join the AA," says Stern.

"What you need is a good butt kicking. This bureau has pride in itself. We take care of our own. Agent Micovich is a fine lady. She made a mistake. You keep your mouth shut about yesterday. It is that simple. Call this number if you have important information. That is the supervisor hot line."

Cliff writes down his number and hands it to Richard. Moses calls for a taxi and waits outside the motel. He keeps thinking about Monica and Stern. Finally, he walks back into the motel.

"Stern, here is two hundred bucks. Stay in this place for a few more days. I'll get back to you."

As soon as Cliff Moses got back to the office, he calls NSA Assistant Director Jake Jeffries, a colleague from Michigan State University.

"Jake, we have been friends since the college days. The more thought put into Virginia Fox, the more you need Agent Micovich. A needed ingredient is missing. You can improve the mission's prospects by adding Agent Micovich. Remember, you met Agent Micovich and reviewed her credentials. You wanted her in the first place," says the supervisor.

"Agents Monica Micovich and Paula Gavalia are paired on most of the work they do. When they work together, positive results happen. Monica is experienced in espionage work, Jake," says Supervisor Moses, clearly stating the facts.

"You are being offered an extremely talented agent. Advice, if you want it, is this Jake. Better include her on the mission. Remember, your first choice is usually right.

"One more thing, Jake; Monica has a way of rescuing a mission when the going gets tough. Your boss would be very unhappy if the mission failed because you didn't have a good supporting cast when one was offered."

"Send Agent Micovich, Cliff. Have her connect with Gavalia, Lady Jane, and Tex Williams. They will bring her up to speed," said Jake Jefferies.

Protecting Richard Stern slipped off the priority list, but Supervisor Moses is still contemplating a move.

Richard Stern returns to the bottle. Self pity rules as he faces mounting depression.

30

A Shot Is Heard

A reunion of sort took place as agents Paula Gavalia and Monica Micovich hugged.

"Jake has agonized about this job. He changed his mind again. He decided to use one more agent in support of the operation," said Tex Williams.

"Everyone, welcome Agent Monica Micovich," says Tex.

Tex took one look at Monica and he was all for adding support. Agent Monica would partner with Tex in support of Agent Jane and Paula. Tex and Monica were about the same age and in excellent shape. Both were older than Jane and Paula. The lead couple would be Agent Jane and Paula. They would have the most dangerous job.

The MPs, Monica and Paula, are back together. Cliff Moses, instrumental in arranging the link, was not around to take the credit, but Monica had more than a hunch he was behind the sudden change.

Monica Micovich was formally introduced to the others. They discussed the operation and talked about the next step as if the group had known each other for months.

"Monica, we have another appointment with Mr. Mahdi tomorrow. Jane is going to be a farm hand," said Paula.

"Jane, it is time to wear a wire. Monica and I will set up off property. We will tap the phone line going to the farm." says Tex Williams.

At precisely eight in the morning Jane and Paula pulled into the Mahdi farm. Monica and Tex Williams drive down the road in a utility van equipped with a bucket and ladders. After pulling along side of a telephone pole, Monica sets the parking brake. Tex uses a ladder to reach the phone termination. He installs a signal recorder and receiver-transmitter to capture communication signal on the line and over the air waves.

An all terrain vehicle drives by as Tex is setting up his equipment. Tex notes the rifle in the back of the ATV.

At the farmhouse, Mr. Mahdi was on the porch ready for them. As before Jane removed her shoes and coveralls. She has a pair of clean shoes with her along with the gas detector. They enter the house and immediately go to the basement door.

"Mrs. Mahdi doesn't have to worry about my shoes, Mr. Mahdi," says Jane.

"There is no Mrs. Mahdi, Jane."

"After we check the gas meter and lines, your new assistant farm hand will be at your service."

"Mr. Mahdi, Paula will stay in the van as a backup in case we have trouble. We never have trouble but the company says if two employees go to a job one must stay in the van with the radio just in case an emergency is detected. We don't always follow that rule. Two of us can work twice as fast but we only have one detector that works. She is going to walk across the road and see if anyone is home. We missed two other houses yesterday, but if you need both of us to work here we can."

Prearranged at eight ten in the morning, Monica signals Agent Paula by vibrating her cell phone. Paula is to ask Mr. Mahdi if he has a cell phone. If he does, they want to lock on his signal and find the farm phone wires if Agent Paula uses his house phone.

Paula walks inside but doesn't find anyone.

Mr. Mahdi closes a second door behind Jane after descending the basement steps. Together they go through a different portion of the basement. Agent Jane has a small pocket light and is cautious and nervous as Mr. Mahdi takes the lead. The light is dim. Hardly enough light is shining from the old light fixtures that are caked with cob webs.

"Where are you going, Mr. Mahdi? It seems like we made a wrong turn." He asks her a question in response.

"Don't you want to see all the gas lines? This old farm has two gas lines that serve the system. I rarely come down here," replies Mr. Mahdi.

"What did you say your last name is, young lady," asked Mr. Mahdi.

"Jane Leford is the name, Mr. Mahdi. The name sounds a little like Lefty. You call me, Lefty, because I'm left handed. It rhymes with Leford a little bit," says Jane.

"Where are you going, Mr. Mahdi?" asks Jane.

Paula is looking for Jane and Mr. Mahdi.

"Mr. Mahdi or Jane is either of you here? Is anyone home? Did you go out a back way?" Paula calls out.

Paula walks ahead and looks in two rooms. She doesn't find a phone. When she opens a door a cat runs between her legs. She almost screams, but bites her hand.

Jane isn't around and neither is Mahdi. Paula decides to go back outside and see where the gas line might feed the farm house. She might be able to look through a basement window. Her watch indicates eight twenty-one.

Jane follows through a dark passageway. Mr. Mahdi enters a dark room. The musty smell of old permeates the air. The ground is dirt and cinder. It is cool and damp.

"We are almost there, Miss Leford. Just one more room and we are there."

Mr. Mahdi turns to Jane and says, "Watch your head. Suddenly, a thump smacks her head. Jane feels her legs go limp as another punch finds the side of her face. She hits the ground as if she were a teddy-bear dropped to the floor.

"Grab her legs," says Mahdi.

Meanwhile, Paula is outside walking to the side of the house when she sees the birds fly into the red barn. She walks closer to the barn to get a better look. The birds look to have tape on a leg.

Agent Tex could see Paula from the vantage point where he was working. She was walking over to one of the farm buildings. She was two hundred fifty yards from them. Paula was near the red barn by a tree with overhanging limbs.

The land has a rising crest as seen from the road. Hay was bundled and laid in the field. A border between the next properties was marked by a row of saplings. Tex and Monica were almost to that point.

Tex finished his telephone work and the two agents pack up and start moving the van. Agent Monica is concerned that no signal can be picked up. She drives the van down the road looking at the end of Mr. Mahdi's property. As she looks to her left side, her eyes become fixed on a person off the road near the edge of the property line. A hunter is inside the row of young saplings that grow by a drainage ditch. He has a rifle raised, pointed toward the Mahdi farm house about four hundred yard away. The hunters view couldn't be blocked. The hay field was cut down. Some trees were dotting the landscape.

"Look Tex, that hunter," she barks.

Tex moves in lightning fashion. He reaches over the steering wheel and presses the horn switch. The van horn billows out a loud blast. A shot rings out as the distracted hunter lowers his rifle to see who's responsible for the noise. He looks back toward the target and quickly checks the fallen person near the barn. He lowers his rifle to see Tex dash out of the van heading toward him.

"Go check Paula, now! Tex, a muscular, black athletic man, runs full speed across the road. The hunter turns away, moving rapidly from the hard charging agent. The one hundred fifty yards separation between the men is covered by spots of heavy brush. A covey of quail take flight as Tex closes rank.

"Stop, Texas Ranger," commands Tex to the hunter.

The hunter, now realizing his security is compromised, sprints through the brush. He jumps a small creek and reaches his off road vehicle. As he does, he throws his rifle into the back of the ATV and quickly starts the vehicle. He stomps on the gas, spinning the knobby tires. The vehicle doesn't take long to reach get-a-way speed. The bouncing ATV flies over a small indent in the trail. In the back of the ATV, the rifle flips from the ATV as he hits a rut in the overgrown trail.

Tex watches as the ATV gains speed and moves out of sight. Tex is no match against the speeding ATV. He slows down having sprinted three hundred yards. He slumps over at the waist trying to catch his breath. He squats down and slumps to his knees. He pulls out his cell phone and calls Monica.

"Monica, is everything alright," asks Tex?

"Paula is down. I'm about fifty yards from her. I'll call you back in a few, she cries.

She drives up the farm driveway. The telephone van skids to a stop ten yards from Paula. Monica grabs a first aid kit mounted between the front seats. She jumps from the van in a hurry to help her fallen partner. As she rushes over to aid her friend she says a prayer to God.

"Please, dear God make her," Paula stops.

"She's moving, God," Monica cries as Paula rolls on her side. Paula moans a little, shaking her head.

"Paula, it's Monica," she says.

"Paula, are you ok?" she asks.

"Talk to me, please, please," she pleads.

"What's going on?" the dazed agent asks.

A small bump and a trickle of blood fall from the right side of her head.

"Someone took a shot at you. We saw a hunter in the field and he was aiming his rifle this way. Tex is after him. Tell me if you're hurt anywhere else."

"I'm ok, Monica," Paula says as she checks to see if the rest of her body can move.

Paula moves her head back and forth. She sits up and bends her knees together. She brings her arms around to hold her legs.

"Wow, I never thought," Paula says, then stopping her sentence.

"I never thought I would be shot. Hey, we carry guns, but really. We are definitely on to something here," Paula relates.

"Agent Jane, we have to find Jane," cries Paula.

"I'll call Tex and let him know you're ok. It's a head wound but I think you'll be ok. Tex might need help. Let's rescue Jane after we get Tex," says Agent Monica. Monica dials Tex William's cell phone. Tex fishes for his cell phone as it call out a tune.

"Tex, this is Monica. Jane might be in trouble."

"Paula is ok. She has a superficial wound on her head. Are you ok?" asks Monica.

"I'm ok. The hunter got away but I got his rifle. Pick me up on the side of the road," says Agent Tex.

"We have to find Jane," says Paula.

"Jane didn't answer when I called for her."

Monica calls Jane to let her know what's happening but doesn't get an answer.

"This is serious," says Agent Paula.

"Mahdi is up to something and I think the birds on this farm hold the answer."

The ATV speeds down the road. The hunter pulls over after he is satisfied he made his escape. He dials a number on his cell phone and explains his situation.

"I escaped but I lost my rifle," he says.

"Mohammad Habbib el Rovi listen to what I say. Find the other cell phone in the glove box. You will get further instructions from the red cell phone. That's the emergency cell phone," says Mr. Big.

Mr. Big continues, "When you have an emergency, I have a backup plan for you. We need to get you out of there. Just dial 300–1234. Then you wait for instructions. You will be sent to another location. We will be waiting for you."

The hunter finds the red cell phone and dials 300–1234. He waits as the phone dials to connect the number. He sits waiting for an answer. The ATV starts to lurch. It was almost as if the ATV came alive. An explosion shakes the ground, launching the ATV. The ATV is sent twenty feet into the air as it is ripped apart by the dynamite. The mangled body of the hunter is deposited off the trail. He looks like an animal carcass run over by freeway cars.

Mr. Big has one more person to check.

"The farm, I need to know. What is happening at the Mahdi farm?" he asks himself.

"Who is tipping these agents?" he asks loudly.

31

Help

"Mahdi, this is Mr. Big. You lost a guard today. Mohammad Habbib, one of your members, was martyred because of his mistakes. American agents are on your farm. How did these agents find your farm," asks Mr. Big?

"American agents must be stopped. If your bird project fails, al Qaeda will be damaged. We cannot afford these slips. You know how to handle this. You must move your bird project ahead. Put members in the field as soon as possible. The Washington attack moves ahead of schedule. You have no time. No days, Mahdi, is all you have left. I will be around to make sure there are no slip ups," says Mr. Big.

The phone clicks and the line goes dead. As Mr. Mahdi hangs up the phone he passes Agent Jane. She lay across the couch, beaten and bloody.

He walks to the window and ponders the situation. He covers his head trying to forget the mistake his friend Mohammad Habbib made. He calls for his guard.

"Ravi, are you here?"

While he is turned, Agent Jane has dialed her partner.

"Help," the voice calls out.

Mahdi slaps the phone away. He gives an upper cut to her chin. She collapses to the floor. Her feet are gathered together and she is carried to a bedroom downstairs. Blood drips from a wound on her chin. Dazed, she realizes two men are pulling on her clothes. She grabs one of the men and as she does a fist slams to the side of her face.

"This is bad trouble, drive," billows Tex.

"I know! I know! I heard a call for help," says Paula.

As if starting a race, Paula has the van moving ahead. The team prepares for battle. She steers the van with her legs as she draws her weapon. Instinctively, she chambers a round into her gun.

The van pulls into the farm drive. It doesn't take long for the agents to reach the front of the house.

"Cover me," says Tex as he jumps from the van and barrel rolls to the first porch step. Monica has the van door open and uses it as a shield. Her gun is pointed at the farm house door.

"I got the back door," yells Paula as she shifts the van into park. Paula runs next to the house keeping her back against the house siding. As she moves along she avoids the window area. She stops near the back hand railing and peers ahead. A slight motion is seen and she waves to Monica. Paula points with a finger to the area inside where she saw movement.

Monica waves to Tex and whispers.

"Back, back door," she says.

Tex springs to his feet and dives onto the porch. In a forceful kick, he breaks the front window. He slides across the porch and kicks another window ten feet to the right of the front door. Silence prevails after the glass settles to the floor.

Suddenly, a single gun shot blows a hole through the front door. Tex leaps over the banister to the ground. He runs to the side of the house and peeps through a window. The living room is empty. Monica watches him move like a cat. He scales the tripod mast holding the roof antenna and leaps to the front roof. In a bold move, he crashes through the upstairs window. Inside he darts from room to room checking for the terrorists. He finds the stairwell leading downstairs and slowly descends a few steps. He can see the front door below. Instinctively, he leaps to the first floor and aims the Glock semi-automatic pistol. A terrorist exposes his head from a room down the hall. Tex fires one shot striking the man in the head. The terrorist drops his weapon and falls dead.

Tex reaches and opens the front door and motions to Monica. His finger points, one down. Tex moves in a bear crawl along the hallway until he reaches the body of the fallen terrorist. He picks up the man's pistol and puts it into his waist band.

Tex looks inside using the dead man as a shield. Jane is lying on a bed. Her face is bloodied and bruised. Her shoes are off and one leg of her pants is removed. She's not moving but Tex can see her chest heave.

Tex looks around the room eyeballing everything. His searching eyes find two shoes of a man behind the drapes. Two doors inside the room are closed. A hanging fan spins slowly making a slight whine. The clock on the wall indicates one eleven in the afternoon. He fires three shots into the tan drape and watches the shoes lift off the floor.

The drape is grabbed by a falling body as it crashes to the wood floor. The terrorist's gun drops and spins to a stop a few feet away. Tex reaches for the hand gun and pushes it to the far side of the room. He moves near the first closed door.

Gun shots ring out as another terrorist bolts from the back door. Paula fires nearly point blank. Her accurate shots trip the man. The terrorist does a one and half summersault and flattens out. His motionless body starts to stain the ground blood red.

Tex turns the handle on the first door. He squats low and lets the door open slightly. His fingers pull the bottom of the door open to reveal a closet. The closet is empty except for a wood hanger. Tex grabs the hanger and uses it to knock on the next door. Tap, tap he knocks. There is no answer. He opens the door. Inside it leads to another room where a propane tanks is standing in the middle of the room. Attached to the tank is what looks like a timing device.

"Agents clear out, a bomb, a bomb!" Tex screams. In a heroic act, he races for Agent Jane. He finds her wrist and sweeps her up in a firemen's carry. Her dangling pants leg flips around in front of them like a flag in the wind. Tex is moving at breakneck speed with Agent Jane across his shoulder. He makes it to the open front door and kicks the screen door open. The one hundred ten pound Jane is a feather to the muscular Texan. He dashes across the porch steps as the farm house lifts off like a space shuttle. The two agents are nearly clear of the blast. The force of the blast lifts them. They're propelled away from the farm house. The extra momentum is God's hand at work. He sends them to the edge of the small pond in the front yard.

The cool water stimulates Agent Jane. Her bruised and bloodied face is able to muster a slight smile as Tex holds her against his chest. Monica and Paula race over to the two exhausted agents and form a team huddle. Monica and Paula affectionately hold Tex as if he just threw the game winning touchdown.

The propane tank was launched like a missile. The flying tank with its nozzle of gas spreading a fire trail in the air crashes through the barn roof. It starts a massive hay fire that cascades to the chicken coop. The fire causes a domino affect that burns cages of birds. The stored chemicals in the barn, that were to be used in the Washington, DC massacre, are incinerated in an act that could only be attributed to America's Savior.

The terrorist's laboratory, bird sanctuary, and farm burn to the ground. Terrorists inside the inferno burn as well. The American team of crime fighters added more distance from the fire as they watched from the far side of the pond as pigeon, doves, and exotic birds made failed attempts to exit. Some chickens had freedom to roam the farm and they did flee the scene in good order as if ordered to evacuate. The fire gave new meaning to fried chicken, as torched birds were catapulted into the air by exploding propane cylinders. So intense were the flames; that nearby trees were reduced to leaf-less trunks of seared bark.

Safety forces arrived within ten minutes, much too late to knockdown the raging inferno. They rolled out hoses to the pond and the fire truck pumped water far too late to save any of the buildings.

The crime fighters climbed into the back end of the ambulance unwilling to separate from the gurney prone, Agent Jane but, the EMS commander ordered the uninjured agents to follow in the backup station wagon.

A second response team arrived. Their fire station captain followed in his station wagon to see a spectacular fire. Hissing cylinders of gas explode and bottles burst. The intense heat radiates skyward on a windless day. Multiple colored objects burst into the air. He thought to himself.

"The Star-Spangled Banner was written when viewing a scene like this."

The End

Looking Ahead

The final novel of the trilogy answers remaining questions. For Richard Stern, he is soaked in self pity. He finds his one night fling has consequences. The bottle is still his answer but Father Pete and Paula offer an avenue for recovery. That recovery is short circuited as Agents Roman and Wright receive new orders from Supervisor Moses. They have Stern in tow as Moses decides he must use Mr. Stern's habit as his trump card for fighting terrorism. Stern hits the bottle and his use of alcohol helps extend his streak of terrorist busts. Unfortunately, one of the agents is mortally wounded.

Monica is faced with a growing problem. She finds out her past error leads to greater complications. She attempts to bond with one of the agents as a means to help shield her and have a fatherly figure around. Trying to lasso Bill Wright is quite the task for Monica. Wright, a ladies man and adventurer, hardly fits the role. He leads his partner into a terrorist trap because of his risky crime fighting zeal.

Captain Awad and Mr. Big are not through with the Great Lakes area. Their connections in Detroit and Toledo convince them to try a new operation. A Texas border adventure receives cooperation from the Mexican government.

The FBI team celebrates in Cleveland because of the outstanding operation. The party atmosphere offers Monica a chance at romance and a father.

NSA Agent Jane recovers from her injuries. Jane and Tex are called upon again as the terrorists refuse to surrender. Boating skills are required as al Qaeda plans new mischief.

978-0-595-44434-2
0-595-44434-2

Breinigsville, PA USA
06 July 2010
241286BV00003B/15/A